THE EXPERIENCES OF
COLIN SHAKER

Marcus Tay

COLIN SHAKER is not happy with his life...

He is stuck in his community, and his house. Even though he is one of the most popular kids in school, he still wishes for a more exciting and interesting life where there is something new every day that could occupy him. But Colin is not getting close to his dream life at all when he makes a decision that could potentially change his life. This soon triggers a series of unfortunate events, and things are then adjusted. Colin quickly finds himself at odds with just about everyone else in his surroundings, including his parents. Will he eventually lead a life full of wonders and dreams? Or is he going downhill.

Author: Marcus Tay (13 years old)

Printed in the United States of America

ISBN #: 978-0-9964830-7-0

Contents:

Chapter One: An Introduction

I forgot my goggles, and I regret not having a pair of them clutched in my hand, squeezed together between my fingers, and swinging by my side.

In fact, I have been experiencing splitting headaches since getting bonked-on by the handle of a hammer.

And guess who was carrying it…my non-robotic-programmed-to-stand dog named Kaley. She was rather…creepy, and was *invented* by my own parents…who are MAD scientists. I always wished they had a better job.

My parents are *strange,* and I know being their only son and telling you that without them knowing…is pretty rude.

That is…if you ever run-into two people called Mr. Shaker or Mrs. Shaker, I beg that you don't report to them my opinion. Anyway…they are wise enough to not listen to you…ok?

Further information will not be needed until later…when necessary.

Let me introduce myself. My name is Colin Shaker. I live in a single-family house in Oregon at the little tip next to the ocean.

I get bullied much by bigger boys who call me Colon, a word which can either mean the punctuation, or the large intestine in a human body. It might be because they are jealous that I have all the girls on my side.

I am adored by every girl who has ever seen me walk-by even though my last name is sort-of funny.

It's very weird that I have no friends that are boys…but simply too many in the opposite gender. Truth is…I don't even put gel in my hair, well maybe sometimes, but not often or constantly.

I find it very annoying that random girls just call my home-phone and ask for me through my parents.

How did they know the phone number? It's still an enigma to me nowadays. I always start saying 'Yes miss?' and then hang-up.

You might think that I'm crazy by not trying to have a chance with these girls, but just to notify you, I'm highly not interested in romance. Or maybe I do a tad. In any case, I seriously want to stop the deluges of phone calls. They are annoying and wasting my time, honestly.

Our neighbors are extremely not-nice. They love to climb-up ladders and drill holes in my house's quartz wall…from the outside obviously. Before long, that had to stop, I assure you.

My parents have tried dialing Homeland Security, but whoever was on the phone just assumed that our neighbors were taking revenge on us and told us to deal with the matter ourselves.

We have considered moving…but the bank refused to let us because my parents didn't pay down the mortgage.

And a result of having neighbors drill holes in our walls was having mosquitoes entering the living room and biting us from every angle.

We even found a few dead in our dishes of food. Thanks to that, now I only eat platters without sauce and steamed veggies.

Back to the present.

My mom and I decided to go take a swim and have some time to dip our heads in cool water. What I always wished was not getting into any trouble with anyone anywhere. But unfortunately, that is simply impossible…no doubt.

"Colin…don't you think it's a beautiful day?" mom asked. "I believe so…mom," I replied, blinking my eyes. "Have you been exchanging words with Rhoda Hilda?" mom questioned curiously.

"What? Oh-no, mom, of course not! She's too loquacious," I responded. "Can we please not talk about this?" I added.

I knew that my mom wasn't going to drop the subject, but would continue to elaborate. I waited for two long seconds as I walked. Surprisingly, she didn't say anything. I knew better than to bring-up a different topic. I simply kept my own mouth shut.

Birds tweeted all around us, hiding below leaves. I glanced at my mom, and saw that she was only looking forward, not taking some time to observe her surroundings.

We finally reached the pool's entrance, and I walked into the men's side as mom signed-out the sheet of paper the assistant lifeguard gave her. I didn't feel like going into a public space, but mom's ways rule-over mines. Things always change when she is around.

With flip-flops on, wacky noises kept coming from where my feet stepped-on. It was oddly annoying, but quite fun to do…actually. I continued like this until settling on one of those strap-benches.

The day was steaming-hot…and sure was I desperate to dive into shallow water. I looked around and saw that there weren't any slides to slide down.

From that, I knew many kids weren't going to come because most of them would be enjoying their time in a waterpark or something rather than in a basin of only water. They would consider waterparks 'better' than the usual. For me personally, I would do anything to earn a reward of submerging my head underwater for at least several seconds.

A few feet away, mom finally got out of the ladies-room.

She seemed as if searching for me with her hand to her forehead, shading her eyes from the sunlight that beat down on everybody there.

I waved a hand to signal her that I was in fact present, and wasn't kidnapped as many parents would assume and start worrying. I sighed as she hurried to me.

"Well...take-off your shirt and hit the..." mom started.

"I know...just let me *feel* the atmosphere," I replied hastily, a tad irritable.

I cooled-down slowly as mom checked if we had everything we needed.

Mom knew that she had to stop ordering me to move-around as I tossed my head to the side and cracked a knuckle in my neck.

Mom shrugged in return, dumped our belongings on a circular table under an umbrella, strode to the edge, and cried, "Cannonball!"

She made a large SPLOOSH and a SPLASH. I watched quickly and got myself a good nine feet away.

I stared at the water...which I know has had chlorine added to it. Then I thought of Caribbean water...and my visit to an island in the Bahamas. Both the brightness in color looked awfully at the same standard.

I stood awkwardly as mom continued to call-out at me to get in. I finally obeyed her at last, fast-walked to the curb, and jumped-in from where I was. Cold liquid brushed against my skin, and I automatically hugged myself.

The sensation didn't end until a minute later…while I kept waddling.

Just when I was about to settle-down, I scraped my toe against the like-sandpaper floor of the pool.

I screeched in pain. Mom wisped-around some-feet away, looking apprehensive. I put my hand in the air and made a go-away motion. Unfortunately, mom wasn't convinced that I was simply okay. Maybe it was because she was afraid that I would get a scar.

"Colin…I don't want to be shooed-away, you know that I care for you!" Mom said as though I didn't take it seriously.

"You can see that I'm not a kid anymore…but a preteen!" I cried-back. "That is so…impertinent!" mom yelled, a tad softer.

According to mom, what I said was offensive, and that is very true. She broke-apart. I wanted to comfort her…but how?

"Col…col…my dear Colin, how could you do this to me?" mom asked. Her hands were on her closed-eyes. I decided to let my mom be alone for some time…so I didn't reply.

I have learned not to respond, for my words are always hurtful…and will make any situation worse. Then, I took a deep breath and plunged underwater.

Without goggles on, I still tried to open my eyes. Everything was blurry, and a fraction of a second later, I was breathing oxygen again, controlling how fast I exhaled and inhaled. I didn't dare make eye-contact with mom. I wondered if she was still in the pool.

I spotted the center of the pool and did breast-stroke (or frog) towards it. When I got there, I turned-over to my back and faced the sky. I tried to make-out shapes from different clouds, but couldn't find-any that resembled to anything stored in my brain.

Fifteen minutes passed, and then, it was time to-go. Mom had recovered from her sadness and was acting-out her part as usual by talking to herself cheerfully. I kept quiet.

Chapter Two: The Lab

We walked all-the-way back to our home. "Let's visit your dad, A.K.A. my husband!" mom suggested. I merely protested.

You see, my parents actually have their own company, but after hiring a helper...that guy was quickly promoted from rank-to-rank, and before you know it, he was the head-boss. Just to notify you...the head boss is called Floyd Gordon, and he has a nasty temper. That is why my parents have to work more than sixteen hours a day even though it's illegal.

If they refused, Floyd Gordon can either make you blind by blowing current after current of wind into your eyes with his own mouth, or scratch you up with his four-inch nails. He's cruel, and too powerful to bring-down or go-against.

But today was different. Floyd Gordon has been fired by the government by force. Months ago, my parents had complained about him to the police.

So first...the Sherriff Department sent somebody to pretend to be Floyd Gordon's high school buddy, and after he got his email, he tried persuading the head-boss to resign.

But Floyd wasn't a fool, and didn't accept any deal his fake-friend offered. Then, the government had to call-in OPD (Oregon Police Department) to break-into his work-place and drag him away.

I heard that a few officers were bitten in the process a week ago. And more good news, the judge sentenced Floyd to twenty-three years in prison for excessive madness.

Also, a typed-letter came saying that he is having animal-treatment…like being tamed. Anyhow, he is out of the way, and not an obstacle to my family anymore…which is a relief.

I felt extremely and very good knowing that he was paying his debt.

I'd wanted to meet him in person, but that wouldn't be a great idea, I know. It was so obvious that he doesn't want company. Floyd isn't one of those who can socialize and mingle comfortably. Besides, I'm not in a real hurry to see if his face is ugly or decent.

Today was a great day to wander outside and go bicycling…but mom was more anxious to see dad, and how he progressed. "What about you go…I want to stay home and make myself comfy," I suggested back.

"Oh, sneaking-away to the mall to meet your girl…" mom narrowed her eyes. "Again? No way, that won't happen," I assured her.

"Besides, why would I do that…and arrive at a public space?" I added.

"Colin, I know you…you're an attention seeker!" mom said. "Of course…not," I stuttered, my voice cracking.

"Wow, I was just joking…and you didn't even realize?" mom asked in disbelief. "Anyway, don't be shy, Colin…do what you need to do," mom added. I shook my head violently.

"Huh? I thought you were going to be all-in for it!" mom looked surprised.

"Nope!" I replied.

"Ok…then let's head to your father's workshop!" mom announced.

We walked and talked back home. Finally, the driveway on the same property as the house we lived in, was under our feet. Mom took out her keys and clicked a button on it. A vehicle on our left responded with a noise.

Our transporting car is actually a turtle covered with plates of metal so that other people won't freak out at the sight of him.

The armor also serves a purpose of keeping-secret his identity. Nonetheless, having metal plates over the turtle won't spark-up suspicions.

The reason this turtle can move faster than a simple race car, is because an enormous tubed-engine was fixed to the top of his shell. Plus, each of the turtle's limbs have circular blades stuck at the bottom as wheels.

You might think...would the roads get scared, then? Apparently, that's not the case. Also, the turtle is called Ben the Brawny, even though he really isn't.

An interesting fact is that, my parents created him. They were always blubbering about how the future would bring them fame.

They talked about how animals would be the key to humans enjoying their life by making them slaves. Therefore, running-low on oil won't be a problem if their idea was implemented.

Everything my parents make are from the lab. I rarely visit the lab, to be honest with you, no kidding.

We rode from hilltop to hilltop in Ben the Brawny. At certain times, I could hear our turtle snorting because he was gathering strength to ascend a steep hill.

And when we arrive at the highest point of the hill, he would just slide-down. I used to think that was fun, but not anymore.

I always tried to keep myself as a rock and not go SMACK on the passenger seat in front of me when we descended…but it was hard.

You might think why I'm not sitting in the front. It is because mom worries that if I do, and out of nowhere, an animal's corpse come into sight, I would receive nightmares. A fact is, her superstitions are unpredictable.

After 45-50 minutes, we went into a forest the size of Brooklyn. Almost no sunlight (or shafts and rays) could penetrate the leaves above. They obscured the view of the sky. I knew this because I was looking-through the sunroof when all of a sudden, everything turned dark.

Another forty minutes later, it cleared, and the sun beat-down on us again. A misty gray and brown mountain touched the clouds in front of us. I exclaimed in wonder. The summit rose to a great height, I could barely see it.

The mountain was all rock with the exception of several glass windows close to the center. They were more to the bottom too.

Anyway, what was strange was that no lights shone from within. It was clearly spooking me out.

My parents have no employees working for them, so I was looking forward to being with the closest-members of my family in an awesome place. I have heard of many underground labs, but never a built-in one.

Mom didn't order Ben the Brawny to park himself in a garage. In fact, there wasn't one. She told him to just stay-put at a nearby and circular cul-de-sac.

Before Ben was put into work-mode, dad had given him a patient-potion he made by putting oyster sauce, vinegar, and ranch dressing together. Believe it or not, it actually worked on him. I am guessing that he added a type of liquid chemical in it too…without telling me.

I hopped-off the curb of my car-door. Mom was quicker than me, so I had to catch-up. We headed towards a gate nicknamed 4-Panel Revealer. It is silver. It is basically an enormous door that could be mistaken as a garage one that opens with four different parts sliding to the side into gaps.

14

The doors went downwards, and then in. I wiped my brow with a cloth from my zip-able pocket.

When you look at it from the exterior, there are no lines that separate a part from another. Thing is, you can't tell, and that is what's interesting.

The afternoon was rather chilly, but now, in the evening, it was somewhat hot.

Weather seemed to be getting more and more abnormal by day.

Just saying, my favorite season is fall...and it's not because of having the option to make leaf piles, but because I love raking.

To me, it's not a chore, and I don't even get paid for doing the job. In this rural and wooded place, we get more leaf-fall than snow-fall. Whenever mom opens the brick door when she takes her leave, an extreme number of dried-out remains of leafs come pouring in and flooding the house to the height of a grown man's hips. That's not the end. After the incident, any insect you can imagine scurry-out of their hiding places and scramble everywhere.

Inside was a tiny dark room with a triangular shaped auto-elevator and mosaic on the wall and ceiling. I always pointed out to my parents that it was a waste of time to become unique, but they totally ignored me every single time.

There weren't any 'up' or 'down' buttons, so me and mom just stepped into it. As I said, the elevator works automatically, and before I finished a snap, it…didn't elevate.

Instead, I felt myself fly upwards, and then I suddenly went forward with something solid hitting my back into a worn-out mattress. I exclaimed, "Aughk!" I felt dizzy, and slid to the floor.

"Why did you do that?" mom questioned me, and by the look of her face, I knew she demanded an answer. "What?" "Snap down there! It's offensive!" "Oh…I didn't know," I replied honestly.

"Of course you knew!"

"Seriously, mom, I didn't lie to you," I spoke slowly.

"Don't say that, I don't believe you!" mom screamed, rather loud and ear-damaging. I simply sighed.

Mom was never a fan of long disagreements and body language.

"Uh…why…?" Mom didn't seem to want to change subject, but she did anyway. "Springs!" she muttered. "What?"

"One below our feet down there and another in the side behind us," she jutted her thumb at an area behind me. I twisted my head around and saw what she was talking about.

"Where's dad?" I abruptly asked. "Follow me," mom sort-of ordered.

As we walked, we passed-by a place called Eraser-Marks Engineering and Development Experimental Lab. That is when multiple questions came to me. I asked mom the first one.

"Isn't this built-into-mountain indoor and lonely building a whole single lab?"

"Look around you…" mom suggested.

I did and said, "So many smaller labs are clumped-together into this spot?" "Yes, that's correct, yup," mom concluded.

"Tell me about this part right here," I pointed to the EMEDEL. "You wouldn't need me to explain," mom answered appraisingly. "Why…what do you mean?"

Chapter Three: A New Invention

Somebody gripped my shoulder. I turned around, it was dad.

"Father!" I exclaimed. He smiled his usual smile and hugged me. Don't mention this…but I like my dad more than mom.

"What about I take him around and give our son a tour?" dad suggested to mom. She agreed…and off we went.

"Ok," he said. I knew that dad was going to start lecturing me…which I'm really fine with. "Go ahead!" I urged.

"Do you know that erasers are made from either vinyl or synthetic rubber?" "No…" I replied. Dad swallowed.

"These material are also found in chewing gum…believe it or not!" he continued. I was taken aback. "Seriously?" Dad nodded.

"Recently, an idea sprang into my mind to attempt to find a way erasers can be made edible," dad said to me.

"You do have a wild mind!" I assured him, managing a grin. I tried to seem happy to the best standard I could handle.

"What other projects are you up to now?" I asked randomly. "It's a finished one, come…let me show you," dad responded.

He opened a door and we entered a large room with natural light flashing in.

Then, I saw the enormous windows on the other side. "This is the main lab…?" "You're right!" dad replied.

He led me to a cylinder-shaped piece of hide standing there on a black table-top. My curiosity grew. What is dad going to show me?

He put his hands close to the cylinder and then lifted something out of thin air. A transparent glove shone in the air.

Dad had a proud expression.

"Voila!" "What is it?" the words slid between my lips as quickly as possible. "Oh…nothing much," dad replied, staring at the transparent glove.

I spotted a mold, and his eyes followed mines. He picked it up and spoke.

"The world used to only be able to trap water into a shape…but I, the scientist of all the others, has trapped air for the first time!"

Dad sort of screamed rather than saying it in an announcing tone.

I even made this visible!" he held up the glove. Dad was overwhelming himself, I thought. He surely was.

He studied me and said, "Put it on, you won't feel a thing!" I offered my hand…and he dropped the glove into it delicately. The material was elastic.

It felt jiggly.

I was ready to yell out the fact that I could actually *feel* the gloves inside cover rubbing non-aggressively against the smooth skin of my hand that I was shaking in the air to test.

But half-a-second later, all the feeling seemed like it died-away except for a single piece of thread drooping on what I thought was my pinkie.

"There's a typo…it's not perfect," I pointed out. Dad looked sad all of a sudden. "No! I didn't mean that…I was just joking!! I responded vigorously.

His expression brightened up…which no doubt surprised me.

"Ah…don't worry too much, you seriously believed the truth was lying on my face…I got you pretty good," dad said calmly. My shoulders fell from the sides of my neck.

"I thought I insulted you!" I said loudly. "Now, now, I kept that piece of string there intentionally!" Dad explained.

"What had you mean?" "It's complicated," dad said, looking away. "No…no…I can understand!!" I begged. "That's my son," he replied and continued.

"That piece of fiber is like a thumb-drive," he spoke nonchalantly. I felt whacked on the head by a mallet, and that it hurt so much that I couldn't feel the pain or suffer…which was in a way good, not counting internal bleeding.

"For what?" I asked. "Basically for stealing clean types of writing…" dad tapped his shoe against the floor and started whistling. "Excuse me? Listen…I don't get it…" I trailed off. I was kind of angry somehow.

Dad sped through his words. He was pretty embarrassed, and I knew that just from observation.

"There will be a new era, a new society, and a new way of life!" he'd cried.

That got my attention. "Everybody will pay by scanning there handwriting rather than using plastic credit cards so as for everything else! This will be a good investment for me and I will accomplish my goal of earning one quadrillion," dad talked swiftly. He was getting over-excited, and that wasn't good.

"But why heist other people's writing type?" I questioned demandingly.

"You see...I'm going to send you on many missions..." "Why don't you go yourself?" I questioned again.

"You're a kid," dad said automatically. "It will be harder for me to get through narrow and tight places...and you're faster than me when running...so the job will be done in almost no time!" dad answered cheerfully.

"Here, we will discuss this later. But you and I have a party to attend! We are going to celebrate!" dad started strolling out the main lab. I reluctantly followed him.

Chapter Four: Time Killin' at the Bar

Dad and I rode a bus to the center of a town called "Smackeder-naturack." I'm pretty sure I know what you are thinking right now.

It isn't a very legit name, but when the idea went to the governments', they were worried it would add to their tedious list of national problems to address. So, the name passed as 'Very Reasonable'.

The real translation is 'Smack-Under-Natural-Rock' but citizens (like mathematicians) were too lazy and not in a mood of such a long name.

The place was designed for only teens, but dad and his team promised to pay double plus triple tax. The manager agreed, obviously. Who would reject such an offer? I mean, would you really do that.

First of all, I need to introduce a few people to you before it's too late. This is a must before you meet them. This is something like a warning so don't skip the page and the one after (deep breath) here I go.

A girl I mentioned before, Rhoda Hilda, is a garrulous person. She loves to get into trouble with random people.

Rhoda can literally go up to somebody in a restaurant and act as a 'straw man'. She would scream at them with accusations and complaints. Rhoda didn't need to gather stuff to blurt out. It was all automatically.

Second of all, there is a little boy named Bernard Dirk. He is six years younger than me. His vocabulary is no good.

Also, Bernard has a *belief.* He never trusts any chair. He never sits down. If you tell me this, I wouldn't believe you, but it's the truth. Instead, lying down has replaced it ever since he acquired the idea three years ago.

One time, at school, I sat on him in the cafeteria as he rested on one of those benches. I was too distracted by our mascot walking in and saying hello.

Everybody just erupted in laughter, yelling…you name it. From that instant on…I've learned to keep a distance from the boy because my rear end still aches till this day.

Also, when I jumped up, my belly hit the edge of the table. So that was a negative bonus too. Embarrassment & Humiliation are my biggest fear. They are something I try to avoid very corner I turn (literally or not).

A third person is another girl called Audrey Beryl. She has feelings for anything tangible. For example, school supplies, etc.

Audrey would literally won't allow you to throw an item away even if it is covered with cobwebs. But the weird thing is…if you tell her she has problems, several blows to your face is possible.

Lastly, there is another girl named Kirsten Dawn. I'm actually pretty soft on her. The only things she has I don't like is that she criticizes how a person, place, or thing appears. Basically the nouns of the world. Also, she's in love with nature, but is anti-technology.

And guess what, I'm about to visit them all at a bar called Intensity Increase of Drinking. I often dub it IID. Why not? Everything these days are short-formed.

Dad and I entered and a lady stood there behind a podium. She showed us the way, picking up a handful of menus.

The strange thing is…she didn't ask how many were coming. Maybe she didn't have any experience of asking. Anyway, dad had already said friends were expecting him there. She nodded her head.

Champagne was lined up on the wall, in opened-up pantries. TV was at every corner of the bar. They were mostly displaying live sport games that I had no interest in. Teens sat on high chairs, chatting with each other. Blue light shone here and there.

A waiter behind the 360 square counter accidentally dropped a bottle of wine. It shattered on the floor. People gasped. He said he was okay. Then, the teens went back to their dilly-dallying. I ignored them.

Somebody popped-out a piece of cork. I kept my focus forward. I heard some teens crying-out at me for no reason. I didn't dare face in their direction…or look at them.

I heard something about a challenge. Maybe they wanted me to be involved in a rap battle. As a little kid, I would have thought it was a cool thing to do. But I'm not a fool anymore.

Then I saw them…people I knew. They were standing there with much style, wearing jeans and collar-less t-shirts.

Their hands were in pockets. Their faces radiated seriousness. But the expressions changed as I got closer.

"*Hey,* Colin!" Audrey proclaimed.

"Audrey!" I didn't know how to continue. Kirsten blocked my way and pulled me into a hug. I widened my eyes and said thanks.

Rhoda stuffed a neatly-folded piece of paper into my hand. "Read it when you get home...I don't want anyone to know except the people I want to invite."

I was tempted to open it and find out about the secret.

And then, I spotted one other girl who I met before. She was the prettiest of all but I really didn't know how to greet her. I took my place across from her in the booth.

I turned my attention to the menu and made it stand on the table with my hands gripping the sides as though it was a wall so the girl wouldn't have to see me. I was reluctant with looking at her but maintained my calmness by studying the menu and the entrees on it. I turned to the beverages and read the names of the alcohol and beer. I wanted to try some but wasn't of age yet. It was too bad. I turned my focus to the appetizers and desserts sections.

I barely noticed myself licking the sides of my lips. I decided to just order nachos with a spinach cheddar dip.

The waitress brings it to me and sets it down on the table. Kirsten walks over and sits next to the unknown girl. "Oh my gosh, these are amazing!" she takes her hand to lift up a chip, then scoops some of the spinach cheddar dip.

Then, after hearing her eat the chip, Rhoda and Audrey came over to join the club. Audrey swooped in and sat next to me. Rhoda stood there in front of the booth with her arms crossed like she wasn't enjoying this.

"What's your name?" I asked the mystery girl who also had her menu up as though she had the same idea as me.

The girl pulled her menu down. "Why do you want to know?" she raised her eyebrows. I started getting agitated.

I gave a very dumb response. "It is just for my information…" I trailed off, regretting the answer.

She sighed and said, "Florence, nice to meet you. I just moved here and my dad is an entrepreneur who is in a business meeting right now. He figured that this bar would be a pretty nice place to have one with one of his business clients along with his partners and associates. I live in North Fields."

"I am also going to attend Tony Craig Middle School," Florence added. I couldn't control it, but my jaw dropped. The new girl was going to attend my school in fall.

"What?" I yelled. "Well, do you have a problem with that?" Florence questioned with her cool voice.

I thought of school with the usual walking around, hitting people you know with the usual "What's up?" I thought about how popular I was on the so-called Famous Spectrum. The popular kids always had friends approach them to talk about who-knows-what. I was pretty famous. Every few steps, someone approaches me and starts a conversation that will end up with me and the person laughing hard. That is why I am always late to class.

Lately, I did not have any guy-friends come talk to me. Probably, it is because of my popularity increasing with the girls. I bet the guys are pretty jealous of me and my physical appearance. Just maybe. I bet they are all waiting for a chance to beat me up when nobody is around except their buds, and get away with it. They do not want to get caught red-handed.

Chapter Five: The Party

I returned home with dad. Mom was sitting on the living room couch. She usually moved around to the dining table, the island, etc. I trudged up the stairs without a word and disappeared into my bedroom, locking the door.

I pulled out the piece of paper that was now crumpled out of my pocket and flipped it open. It read: "Party at my place, 8:30 tonight. My parents are gone for the night. I am secretly hosting a party. Please come! Don't forget!" and that was it. Mom and dad would definitely not let me go, I thought. I need to escape.

8:30 came and I silently left the house through the backdoor without my parents knowing. I knew how to get to Rhoda's house. It was only a few blocks away.

Her house was a massive cookie-cutter.

Mom and dad would yell at me, I thought. I need to promise myself to leave by 10:30 so my chastisement wouldn't be as extreme, I hope. But time management doesn't usually work with me, seriously.

There was a throng of middle schoolers outside her house.

Besides, there were too many heads to count. Behind the windows, I could see different colored lights flashing this way and that. There was music coming from within. And of course, people were flooding into the house.

I appeared over the threshold, and everything was just messy. There is cake, soda, chips, and toilet paper everywhere. Trash was all over the floor too.

Someone crashes into me, and I recognize his face. "Watch it, Colon!" and he laughs with his buds as they walk away.

To me, he was a big ugly bully.

Rap music was playing overhead, and middle schoolers were dancing around with crazy arm movements and body/arm/hand/leg movements that didn't make sense.

People were throwing cups and plates at each other while others pour Coke, Sprite, Dr. Pepper, you name it, on each other's faces. There were puddles of liquid on various spots of the carpet in different colors.

I passed somebody taking a whole bag of chips and dumping the substance into his own mouth. Someone else was chugging down a whole liter of juice.

Most of the liquid went out of his mouth and onto the floor creating puddles. Crumbs were everywhere. The furniture was messed up and not in their designated positions before.

A disco ball hung from the ceiling, rotating clockwise and shining different colors of light that reflected off the wall.

Boys and girls started to get into lines with their hands on the shoulders of the one before them. I was caught into one of the chains and we started moving forward like a caterpillar around the big living room.

Girls were taking selfies with their boyfriends and putting on distracting facial expressions. Then, they put them on Instagram, Snapchat, Twitter, and more, bragging to others about how much fun they had.

Somebody was throwing popcorn everywhere.

Middle schoolers started throwing the cushions of the couches at each other, prompting a friendly fight.

I joined it without second-thought, slamming the pillows into several girls who attempted to hit back at me.

"Pillow fight!" someone cried. I dodged but got hit a few times. People were jumping around everywhere, reaching the ceiling and touching it, and on the ground again, and repeat.

Kirsten and Audrey were besties and appeared next to me. "Hi Colin!" they said together. "Are you enjoying the fun?" I nodded and got back to what I was doing.

Bernard was there. He was Rhoda's little brother. Besides, where was Rhoda all this time? Somewhere in the bathroom?

This was pure exciting.

This was living life the right way. I wanted to do this every day for the rest of my life without needing a job or education or school or college.

A few girls stumbled over and snatched my arms. They dragged me to a nearby couch. I fell onto the middle with girls all around me. They put a pair of sunglasses on my eyes.

"Colin! Say cheese!" a girl pulled out her phone. She pressed the button and took multiple photos with me, adding doggy and cat features on both of us.

A DJ stood in the back in a sound booth, making cool effects.

People all around were drinking, eating, stuffing themselves with unhealthy food, dancing, and having fun.

A few boys were trying to rap in the corner and laughing whenever one of them failed miserably.

I laughed too from my spot at the couch. Then, I felt like the energy was draining from my body because of all the fun.

A girl put her arms around my neck as my eyes drooped.

Another girl went and came back with a handful of chips, soda cans and bottles, cake, and much more. "For you, Colin!" she cheered. She was one of the cheerleaders at school.

I went at the food, chowing down multiple bags of chips, draining countless soda cans, and eating piece after piece of cake. The girls were like my personal servants.

It was like midnight already. I lost track of time and missed dinner at home. My parents must be trying to find me now around the neighborhood and calling people like my principal or dean. I was probably marked missing. They may be dialing 911. But it didn't matter because it felt so good being here. I didn't care now.

Girls were occasionally kissing my cheeks. As I lay down on the couch, a girl pounced on my middle, and I wasn't sure why for real.

I finally lost consciousness and fell asleep.

I woke up on the couch with girls soundly asleep next to me. I slowly opened my eyes and saw middle schoolers all across the floor sleeping, some in the kitchen on the laminated wood. I was beginning to have a stomach-ache too.

I saw grown-ups outside walking up the steps to the entrance of the house into the foyer. Cars were outside.

Some peered in, and one of them was my principal.

My plan was to get up and hide. I tried to, but it was too comfortable here on the couch with girls' hair all over my bare legs. Some slept on my thighs while others' heads were on my shoulders as though they were pillows.

Besides, if I moved, I fear I would wake them up. It was too nice like this. But my fear for the adults was smoldering.

They entered and looked around, shaking their heads. They spotted me and came over. My heart plunged when I say my parents.

I looked up at the furious faces. I grinned, and they said, "Colin, you are so dead!" The principal and dean nodded in agreement. People were waking up and starting to take in the reality. "What is going on? I will find out what was happening last night! I will find out what was happening in this house! You know you guys kept the whole neighborhood awake all night? I got complaints from residents! You will all face severe consequences and be punished! Who invited all of you here?" the principal cried, putting up his arms and looking around, stunned and amazed with eyebrows raised.

"This is crazy!" he added.

My parents had found me, and I'd been busted. Just right now.

One guy raised his hand and opened his mouth. He was going to spoil it. "Her name is Rhoda Hilda, and I do not know where she is right now."

Chapter Six: The Play-Date

"Colin! What were you thinking? What were you doing with girls all over you? How come I never knew you left the house to come to that party? You never got my permission! You are grounded for the rest of the weekend in your room. You cannot leave! I looked everywhere for you! You scared me to death!" Mom yelled at me as I stood there.

"Never again will I keep or let you out of my sight, you hear that? Never!" she demanded. Dad stood beside her with his arms crossed as I stood against the wall.

"Mom! That is merely impossible!" I retorted. "No! Don't talk-back to me! I feel ashamed and shameful for raising such a son. I do not want to hear your voice again!" "Well, what about you, huh? I am pretty sure you did the same thing, if not…" I fired back. "Don't question me like that! I demand respect! Now, into your room!"

I left my place and stomped into my bedroom, closing the door. This was insane. What is so bad with joining a party and trying to enjoy life and have fun?

Mom and dad were wrong. They were totally and completely wrong! I disagreed with them.

If I had to fight for my positions, stances, and opinions, I would work as if I was in a debate on stage.

And so, I spent my weekend stuck in my bedroom without anywhere to go. I was bored to death since because my computer and phone was taken away.

I was left with a few stress balls for my entertainment. How could life be so boring after the experience at the party? The fun at the party was indescribable.

But now, I was bored to death, you know.

I paced the room, sat, ate when mealtime came, used the bathroom, asked for something to drink—water, then tried to sleep, and repeat. Most of the time, I just lay on my bed, tossed the pillows, ruffled the blankets, and squeezed the stress balls.

I started to just concentrate and focus my attention on the design of the hardwood on the floor, and the design on the walls as well as the ceiling.

I kept tapping my fingers on the little night stand in the corner that held my clock. I stared at my desk.

It was too bad my bathroom was attached to my bedroom or else I would have had an excuse to get out.

I had been locked in. I had heard the twist of the lock and it clicking from the metal of the key. I wished I had a pair identical to the same key so I could leave because I was getting desperate.

My heartbeat was rising at the second.

Some spirit in me was driving me to kick-down that door that stood as a solid tangible barrier. But of course I couldn't.

I wanted to crack open and tear up the walls to shreds.

The stomach-ache was growing and hurting more than ever. I really wanted to take some medications but couldn't. I groaned in pain as I stumbled to the bathroom and directly to the toilet. I stopped in front of it. I doubled-down and vomited (barfed) right into the bowl continuously and nonstop for 5 minutes. I couldn't believe I ate that much. I was feeling groggy and washed my face.

Hours passed, and finally the night went by with me soundly asleep even though I didn't use much energy being in my own room the whole day in its entirety.

I heard footsteps shuffle by and a click. The door flew and swung open. I stared at mom from my own bed just in time to hear dad say, "…Teenage problem!" By then, I was wide awake.

"I'm sorry Colin," mom remarked. Dad didn't say a word. "I forgive you…" mom said, and everything went back to normal.

When I was in my room, I was thinking 'how could they do this to me?' but now, it was a whole different story and the complete opposite. All I cared was being relieved to be able to be free again and step out of my room and down the stairs to the first landing. I looked at the calendar and realized it was the last day of summer vacation already. Tomorrow would be the first day of school.

The first day of school was great. Kirsten came over and asked me if I could come over to her house.

I went home and begged my parents, who gave in at the end.

I made my way to Kirsten's house.

It was a short trek.

I stopped at an enormous fence and rang the doorbell. The gates opened and at the end of the field was a massive and gigantic mixed traditional and modern house with several stories. Parts of it like the windows were modern and sleek. While the rest was very traditional.

There were bluestone slabs that composed a walkway through the supreme landscaping into the house.

I walked through the door and saw a man with bulging muscles sitting on the couch with a laptop and the TV on broadcasting a live football game with reporters bantering. He constantly looked at the TV and flickered his eyes to the screen.

He was a big guy and barely noticed me walk in. Kirsten came running past him to me. The big guy got up, putting aside his computer. At that point, I knew he was her dad.

"Hey! Come to my room!" Kirsten cheered.

I followed her and saw a little kid playing videogames in front of another TV. The entry way had high ceilings.

I walked through a kitchen with a stone countertop island and white cabinets. The house was open-concept.

It was full of new stainless steel appliances.

I went through a rec room and a few hallways to the staircase. Kirsten signaled for me to walk up the stairs.

Another set went down to the basement.

I trudged up the stairs one by one reluctantly. At the top was her room. I entered and immediately saw a makeup station with a large mirror. Kirsten locked the door and I gulped, not sure what to do next, or what would come next, or what would happen next.

I didn't know what was in stall for me. I was pretty reluctant.

Kirsten walked over and took my hand, clenching it. I wasn't sure how to react. She put her other hand around my neck.

Then, I felt myself losing my poise and falling sideways onto a king-sized bed that was Kirsten's. I hit the bed with Kirsten on me. She grabbed my head and made me kiss her right away. I couldn't retract. Why did she even need a king-sized bed all for herself anyway? We got to work, kissing madly.

I completely lost my mind, not sure why. You know what I did?

I tore off my shirt to reveal my bare body and pulled Kirsten closer to conserve heat. She seemed as though she was in a trance. Her legs wrapped around my middle and her bare feet touched my back.

It was so comfortable.

We were rolling around on the bed, kissing so much as if I wouldn't need any more water for another week because of all the wetness.

We were clinging and clenched tightly to each other as if we were inseparable. We couldn't stop. We were stuck to each other and grasping each other too. We were smooching too much. We lay there, squeezed together, flesh touching flesh and body touching body.

The door to her room crept open. Her dad appeared with the little kid behind him at his heels. His eyes widened. "Daddy, are they making out?" the little kid asked curiously.

"Kirsten! What do you think you are doing?" her dad cried.

Kirsten hadn't noticed and retracted. She was smiling at me and then she finally glanced behind her.

The sight of her dad wasn't pretty.

Her smile faded, left with a hint of guilt and embarrassment.

Her dad was going to blow. He was going to explode. "Dad, I was just…" Kirsten trailed off and couldn't continue.

I was traumatized, being in the wrong place at the wrong timing. I was cuddled up with Kirsten on her own bed, laying there, and now immediately sitting up. We were facing each other. Kirsten's dad must have no doubt knew something fishy was going on with all the noises we were making from upstairs. I was so humiliated that I couldn't believe what I was seeing or looking at. I couldn't believe my own sight. I couldn't trust my senses. This was awkward and all-out weird. "Out! Out!" her dad yelled. I took a run for it and went to the open window.

Without thinking, I jumped out, down a story, and crashed onto the lawn.

Pain surged through my body but I recovered and ran to the gate, passing through it, and towards the park. I couldn't go home, no way. I decided to go to the park and hide there, in the playground.

For at least the night, I would stay there. Kirsten and I had been exposed. There was no turning back or re-working and changing the past. It had been done. The act had been made. A very embarrassing and private one, now about to be made public.

Chapter Seven: Exposed

The night was tough and hard. I hid in a dark place under the slide and edged into the corner. I held my breath at every shadow, trying to not move a single muscle. I was sweating. Anything could pop out and surprise me so much my heart would leap. I was scared, afraid, and fearful. You pick the adjective! The next day, I went to school empty handed without a backpack and homework to turn in. I couldn't submit an assignment online too because I couldn't get any access to some kind of computer or device. Today was the due day for the project. I passed down a group of big boys talking together near the lockers. "Dude! You know Audrey Beryl, that hot chick? She sent me a vid of Colin Shaker and Kirsten Lake *attached* to each other," one guy blurted. "Oh what? Are you kidding me? They really were? Can I text you? Send me the vid, I want to see it," another guy said. "I can't believe it, they were kissing on a bed, lying down?"

Then, they spotted me. "Hey! It is our bud Colin!" the guy howled sarcastically, breaking into laughter. They all started pointing at me and laughing so much as if they would fall onto the ground, with their squints. "Hey Colin! How's that love affair?" one kid shouted.

I turned around and switched courses. I was going to take the short cut to my first class, but changed my mind quickly.

I walked down a different corridor, and then a different hallway. I was going on a different route.

How in the world did the cool kids know? Was Kirsten facetiming or skyping Audrey during the incident?

I remembered an upright phone on a table next to the bed. I was done. It was over. Now there are rumors.

People were whispering into each other's ears as I passed, gossiping.

They were constantly glancing at me. I was famous in a negative way. No doubt the school adults already know.

Then, I realized I was lost, stepping past an opening full of graffiti.

It took me another 15 minutes after the time my first class started to find the room. People were grinning when I walked in.

"Colin! You are late again!" Mr. Sarpo exclaimed.

I stumbled to my desk.

The teacher turned his back to the board. Fellow classmates started taking crumpled-up paper and throwing them at me. Some fired spit balls.

"You have a test today, a timed one. You get 30 minutes!" Mr. Sarpo informed. He went row to row and passed out the tests.

I hadn't studied or mastered any of the material. I didn't even know anything on it. It was composed of multiple choice, true or false, define in complete sentences, and short answers. I stared, blank. Time went by fast. I was running out of time. I just scribbled and bubbled-in either A, B, C, or D for each question because I had no idea and was clueless the last minute before the buzzer and timer went off. I made very uneducated guesses (random ones). I just went with my gut and instinct, which I don't have anyway. My grades are already very low, most of them Ds and a couple Fs.

When I left the class, someone challenged me to a fight. I accepted and he punched my face. In return, I slapped and smacked his.

I left the fight with minor injuries, a few bruises and cuts.

It wasn't that bad, compared to others I had been in, most of them duels. Some prompted gangs (whole and entire groups of people) to tackle each other. The teachers never cared. They would just walk by as if they never noticed. They would keep their sight forward, always, no matter the situation. It was just what they do, and most of us had adopted to this. The gangs usually picked on new kids, so I felt bad for those who were.

I wanted to say sorry to Kirsten's dad and most importantly, Kirsten herself for getting her into such a situation.

Now the whole school knew.

Kirsten usually had a group of girls flanking her, but this time, she walked around the corner looking miserable and lonely.

"They hate me now! They hate me! Come with me!" Kirsten cried. I went to walk beside her as people gaped at us.

She was staring at the ground. "It is okay, it is fine…" I assured her. It didn't really comfort her much. As I said, we were exposed. My school was voted a 7 out of 10 for the area. It wasn't that bad on a national and state scale. We actually made the cut to be one of the best schools in the state of Oregon.

The principal must have figured as long as Tony Craig Middle School was on the leaderboards, we were decent.

So very true.

Kirsten had insisted that we would make out. She had forced it through and with me. But why would she do that? Why did she do that, the question is? It was a big mystery, and I didn't quite understand. There must be a secret reason or purpose. Did she *like* me? That would be pretty nice and good for me. Did she want a relationship with me? The questions were bugging me in my head.

It must have took her a lot of guts and rehearsing to push me onto her bed, along with herself. It was an awkward moment, but I wasn't in control. I would have freaked out if it wasn't for the kiss that seduced me so much. It calmed and settled me down.

I felt like I was at the place I always dreamed of, where everything was perfect, and would stay like that forever.

It was a good feeling.

Now here was Kirsten, all sad because she lost all her friends.

She must have fallen down the ranks. She wasn't categorized or titled as 'cool' anymore, apparently.

Her eyes were puffy.

She was going to cry in the middle of the hallway, so I knew I had to do something. I took her arms and said, "Kirsten, don't cry!"

"Ahhhhhhhhhh," somebody exclaimed. "That is *so* cute!"

My face flushed red. I was blushing more than I thought. It was immediate and automatic. I couldn't handle it or control it. It was naturally doing it. So much stress! I was beginning to feel nervous, anxious, and agitated.

People were crowding around and watching.

I gave the lamest excuse possible. "I need to use the bathroom…"

Without thinking, I pulled Kirsten into the boy's bathroom, accidentally.

She shrieked when she saw a boy as though he was an alien. I dragged her back out and into a teacher's single bathroom. I locked the door.

"Kirsten! You can't cry!"

"Why? I need to express my emotions. I made a huge mistake with you. Now everyone knows…" she answered, breaking up and sobbing uncontrollably.

She put her head in her hands, sitting on the toilet at the same time.

I waited for her to finish.

She finally did after a long time. My second class had already started. I took a wet paper towel and gave it to her. She wiped her face. "Better," Kirsten muttered.

I unlocked the door and pushed it open. People were waiting for me outside without going to class. Only the nerds did anyways. All the cool and non-weird (normal, which is how they called them) kids just camped out in the bathrooms to play on their phones in the stalls. Uh-oh, I thought. They seized me and brought me to a water fountain, pushing me down. Somebody turned on the water to spray me in the face. It was like waterboarding but in a revised way.

They let me go and I stumbled to the wall, slipping down onto the floor. I wiped my face with my hands.

"Dude! That wasn't funny at all! Don't do that ever again!" I demanded.

My words never bring what the message wants to change. Never. Never ever.

"Well Colon! You are wrong! You don't use the bathroom with a girl. Everybody knows that!" and they all howled with laughter. Kirsten pushed through them towards me.

"What were you doing in there, Colon? I mean, the bathroom," one kid asked. "I'm not going to tell you!" I yelled back. "Ohhhhhhh," another kid made.

The principal appeared and said, "You are all getting community service after school today plus lunch detention. Those hidden cameras tell everything that is true. Don't try to lie. We have got proof for every little bit of needed evidence to support our claim."

"Colin! You get to rake leaves. Todd! You get to pick up the dog poop. Geoffrey, you have to scrape the sidewalks." "What makes me have to do something worse than Colin? This is unfair! This is impartial! Oh! There you go. Vocab word! Do I get extra credit? Do I get candy?" Todd protested and joked.

"I will assign supervisors and monitors," the principal responded.

Todd slumped his shoulders and pursed his lips to show that he was easily defeated.

The principal left and I turned to Kirsten. She had taken out her cell phone and tapped the home button.

A pic popped out with a few faces of boys staring at us. I recognized them. They were categorized as 'bad' in my opinion. But why is it the first thing Kirsten would see every time she turned on her phone and pushed that button at the bottom?

"Hey...um," I started. "What? Just boys, that's it. Why can't I have other *friendships*," Kirsten questioned rather arrogantly. I backed-off, overwhelmed.

She was having multi-relationships. She must have kissed other boys too. I wasn't the only one.

I had felt so special before, but not anymore. I didn't know Kirsten anymore. Wrong phrase. I never knew her. She was mysterious. She was unpredictable.

Other kids started to crowd around me, and they were big and tough boys. I knew the time was up. I needed to escape and leave. I needed to run. I could see the look in their faces.

I ran the opposite direction and the entire crowd followed, sprinting. "Go get him!" Kirsten cried, laughing.

The whole act was to demean me. This was so despicable. I wasn't going to fall for this stuff again. But I was pretty doubtful at that.

I ran, bumping into several teachers and knocking them down. But I didn't care now. I couldn't afford to get beaten up again. Kirsten had filmed and recorded it for this reason so I could be beaten up.

But why would she do that?

It was so *evil!*

I was infuriated, but what could I do alone? I was the victim with all the blame. I couldn't reverse time and make things right again. No way. I will just have to deal with it.

I couldn't make the memory be gone from the minds of those who knew about my act and what I did.

This situation might as well have planned out my future, whatever it might be or lead to. I just have to hope to be prepared and ready. I was done, as I always say. I went into hiding for the rest of the morning by myself.

Lunch time arrived. People all around were screaming at me and throwing their hands and arms into the air. I decided to sit at a girl-ruled table that was somewhat popular.

They were playing truth-or-dare. One girl was dared something I couldn't make out very clearly.

Before I knew it, all the girls' eyes were on me, and by that, I mean every single pair of them down the long table.

The girl who was dared looked at me square, and I could see her face turning the color red. I grimaced somehow, which was pretty stupid in front of so many people. I didn't know what to expect, and if I would be ready and prepared for it. I felt pretty insecure and reluctant.

The girl opened her mouth and said, "Can I be your girlfriend?" I sat there stunned but responded right away. Was that the dare?

I stuttered and hesitated, struggling to get the words out of my mouth. "Yeah, sure, why not?" I accepted.

Girls all around were like "Aw that is so *romantic*," they spoke dreamily, eyeing the dared girl jealously.

I brushed my hair to the side so it would look cool.

"Okay, I go…" I continued the game.

It was the worst darn game in the world, to be honest with you.

I just tagged along because I had nothing else to do.

Groups of boys came over to my table and mocked me, pouring ice-cold drinks on my head and shoulders, along with something unknown and yucky that was *invented* from food mixtures. The liquid substance flew down my body.

One guy kneed me in the groin as I tried to get up. "Hey! That's not nice! Get away, Bosch! Don't you dare hurt Colin like that again!" one girl commented.

A boy reached into my pocket and stole my lunch money, which he evenly distributed with the other guys of the gang. That was when the principal arrived. "Colin! Don't you dare skip lunch detention again! I told you to come down to the library! You were 5 minutes late! Five minutes is a lot! That was when I had enough and came down to get you! Look at what you've gotten yourself in now! Look at what you are doing!" the principal cried.

I didn't mean to…but cussed for the sake of the matter. "I forgot…" I made an excuse, which the principal didn't buy.

"Colin! What did you say? That is bad language, and is prohibited on school grounds. If I catch you again saying that, you *will* be suspended, you hear me? Have I made myself clear? I expect higher of you, a more mature Colin. Now, since you know already, or maybe not. For your info, just follow me, that shouldn't be too hard to do, right? I understand your age and behavior." the principal admonished. She knew nothing about me, I rolled my eyes.

He turned and I followed. People were booing me and making annoying and harsh noises, sounds that sounded, well, bad.

I lifted my head high and tilted my chin so that I would appear confident and not defeated. Everyone in the cafeteria was watching me carefully now.

They were judging me and trying to find a fault in me.

I knew this. I wasn't dumb. I had to deal with it. It was a must.

My principal brought me into a room in the very far corner of school. I spotted Todd and Geoffrey there.

They were smirking at me and I knew deep down in their heart, they'd blamed me for this. I headed to one of the back desk, but the principal said, "Nope! Move to the front!"

The moment my principal bent down to get something from a filing cabinet, probably the remote controller for the screen, I bolted out of the classroom.

Couple minutes later, a speaker went on. "8th grader Colin Shaker is missing. If you are him, please go immediately to the front office and show yourself! We are assigning a search team now if you don't appear in 5 minutes."

It would be crazy to show myself. It certainly wasn't me who was the troublemaker. I just fell for the trick. I was set up, in a way. The adults are having a miss-understanding. But they don't know that because they don't know all the facts. I knew all the facts. Besides, if I had the opportunity to explain, they still wouldn't believe me because of my history and record of lying to people in school.

It would be certain death to turn myself in. No way! That wasn't even an option. I wouldn't stand a chance with the entire school against me, the lone one without a supporter.

Somebody tapped my shoulder and I jumped. As I said, I knew everyone in my grade. I turned to find a boy there.

"Hey, don't worry, I'm with you. I think you are the right one…" he spoke. "Wait, Trevor, is that you?" I asked.

"You are right! That is correct." Trevor was a pretty smart kid who was good in anything, and by that I mean everything. He was good in all sports and a master at chess. He could easily crush the opponent.

I barely talked with him, though, because he wasn't in any of my classes. My school was big with infinite kids. "I want to help you," Trevor came clean with me. I trusted him, somehow. Maybe I was desperate to have a friend at this moment in time of my life. I felt pretty lonely before. But now, I was brighter with Trevor, and I could hear it in my voice. Trevor wasn't part of the weird or mean kids, so that was good. He was an average and medium. He wasn't cool nor unheard of ever. Trevor always wore a hoodie to hide his identity, according to himself.

Someone else tapped my shoulder. "Looks like someone has gotten himself into a lot of trouble," spoke the grinning face of Florence. My eyes widened.

"Florence, why are you here?" I questioned.

I didn't get the answer I was waiting for, but instead, a gesture.

She brought us to a storage facility and utility room, inside of which was full of cardboard boxes and materials.

It was partially empty too.

She shut the sliding door and we nestled on the floor for a few minutes. Trevor got up and went to the door.

He tried it, but it wouldn't budge somehow. Then, the reality dawned on me. We had been secretly locked in.

By that time, I was panicking. Florence was also. She called out at the top of her voice for somebody, anybody.

Then, the lights went off. I couldn't see a single thing. Was I going to be trapped in here for the rest of my life? Who knows how long it would last now? It was already limited according and based on the circumstances.

There was really no way out. The only exit was gone. There was no gap or hole in the walls or ceiling.

After what felt like forever and eternity, the sliding door slid open, bursting and revealing light. I rejoiced.

A teacher crept through and took something out of her pocket, handing it to Florence's outstretched hand.

It was a badge with the word "Congrats" on the top. Florence pinned it to her shirt. "Why did you get that?" I asked.

"Oh Colin, did you know because I found you I got this? Look, I just entered this new school yesterday. I need to get popular like in my old school. When I saw this situation, I seized my opportunity. I told the adults that if I found you, I would bring you here, and in this case, along with Trevor, which was totally unexpected. I positioned one around the corner to keep an eye for me coming back with you and Trevor. Then, I made it look like something terribly wrong happened. And now, this," Florence retorted.

I couldn't believe it. I was set up once again, twice today by two girls.

"I was just kidding, Colin," Florence winked. I instantly felt relieved but knew that was a lie. The teacher seized me and started dragging me out on foot.

"This time, you are coming with me, and their will not be any more escaping," the teacher ordered. Other teachers started catching up and circled around me. I felt like I was the president flanked by the Secret Service. But in this case, it wasn't to protect me. It was to ensure that I wouldn't escape. Trevor was dragged along by Florence. He would get some of the blame, I figured.

I remembered a time when I attended a school and community dance night. As I was pouring myself some punch, I spilled the liquid on a girl's blouse.

That was how I felt now.

I would never forget the incident. I was brought to the House Office, not the main one. There, I was shoved into a plain and ordinary room with a whiteboard and an electronic board. My heart sank when I saw Kirsten there. She was definitely playing the victim. I was mad at her for all this, seriously. Seeing her face, I felt a bit better, though.

That didn't quite make sense. When I saw her, I should have been overwhelmingly angry. But why not right now? Maybe it was because of her pretty and beautiful face that I couldn't resist or stand not looking at.

I was forced to sit down in front of her across a rectangular table. There were also three more tables in the room. One was circular, and stood halfway between the rectangular one and the corner. The other one was a square and stood on opposite side. The third one was on the very same side as the circular one.

I sat on the long end facing her. I preferred to sit on the short one so I would be farther away, at least, but what choice have I got here? What option do I have here?

Somebody shut the door. "Ok, Kirsten, speak. Tell us what happened with this boy, and we will decide who is guilty. Tell us what this boy did to you, or what you did with this boy!" the assistant principal ordered, arms crossed.

When the teacher looked away, she smirked at me with an evil grin. But that was only for a split-second before it was replaced with an innocent expression.

I rolled my eyes. "Hey! Do not do that! That is disrespectful!" the teacher howled. I nodded and muttered, "Sorry."

"Are you going to talk or what? If not, this has been a waste of time!"

"Go!" the teacher urged.

"Colin went to my house unexpectedly and rang the bell on my door. I didn't even know or wanted him to come, anyway! I opened the door and I immediately was surprised. He pulled me up to my room without my permission by dragging me along with my arm. There, I thought we were going to have some fun and play on our phones, but he pushed and tackled me onto my own bed and started kissing my lips and pinching my waists. I couldn't escape under his weight and grip. I couldn't get out of his grasp. When my dad came in, he had the wrong idea. Colin scared me for life! He made me embarrassed today in school. I was bullied multiple times because of him! Colin is a horrible kid, and a terrible boy!" Kirsten unleashed on me. That was a big, final, hard blow to me.

"Colin! Do you have anything to say? Would you like to respond? Would you like to reply?" the assistant principal asked. I shrugged because I knew they wouldn't believe what I would say.

"Well then!" I suddenly knew I made a huge mistake of not telling my account of the truth. I would have had a chance. But know, it was too late. "Colin, I want you to meet directly with Kirsten's parents and apologize for what you did, that is it."

They made it sound so easy. "In person," the teacher added.

They had already assumed that Kirsten was telling the right and true thing, and I was the one to blame.

I was dismissed to my last class of the day, and Kirsten was my classmate. We were working on a project. "Ok, you all get half an hour to do as much as you can on the project. Go move around and consult with your partners. Whatever is not done is homework," my teacher said.

"Do as much as you can, Colin! I bet we can finish it all today so we don't have to worry about it again," my partner Robin clapped my back. He was a productive and good kid who wasn't annoying.

Robin always finished everything on time, also making the products appear to be high quality even though they were created with cheap things. He loved arts and crafts, too. Robin was good at designing something that was visually appealing and eye-catching, something that would certainly stand out. He also won both the Spelling Bee and Geo Bee.

Just then, I saw Kirsten ask and leave to use the restroom.

She had kept her phone in her desk. "I will be back," I told Robin as he went to get some tape, crayons, markers, glue, and color pencils. "Where are you going?" Robin asked. "None of your business," I dismissed.

Kirsten had acted all upset, now it was time for revenge. I went to her desk and sat down, flashing my eyes to the door to make sure she wasn't coming back yet.

I kept the phone inside the desk so the teacher wouldn't see. Besides, the teacher was busy looking at her own computer, probably checking her email or social media.

I pressed the home button, and I was in. I cheered in my heart to see that I wouldn't need to enter and guess a passcode that I didn't know. I went immediately to her photo album, and to the video section.

I turned off and muted the sound and volume, just in case. She had recorded all of them. I pressed on a random one and watched.

There she was in her bedroom with a different boy. Kirsten grabbed him and shove him onto her bed, getting on top of him. I looked at several others, and they were the same thing, with different boys.

I turned the sound on a tad and heard drastic noises from Kirsten as though she was in pain, but enjoying it. I deleted a few videos of her with other boys before I heard footsteps outside in the hallway coming toward the classroom door. Also, I texted a random boy and wrote, "I hate you." I shut it down quickly. I threw and dropped the phone into the desk, hoping that I didn't crack the screen. I looked around and got up, hitting myself against a metal bar on the seat.

I howled in pain and realized everyone had stopped what they were doing and were watching me. Kirsten walked through the door just in time to see me get up away, out, and from her seat.

I took a step backward and bumped into my teacher. "I saw everything," she informed me. Kirsten ran over and cried, "What did you do on my phone? I knew it, Colin!"

Just before, she hadn't spoken to me as though it was a normal day in the class. I hadn't realized my surroundings. I was too in depth in the activity.

"That is enough! That's enough!" my teacher roared. Kirsten grabbed a nearby desk, pushed it into the air, and charged at me with the bottom of the legs of the seat pointing at me. I screamed. She threw it at me and I was knocked to the floor.

This was going to be another so-called 'epic/special event' that people were going to ask each other about. They would be like, 'did you hear about that?' This would be the headline that people were going to talk about for a long time.

"Stop! Stop!" the teacher cried.

I was the only boy who got into trouble, so why were the others not in the same situation as I was in now?

Chapter Eight: The Rival Teams

I was yelled at by my parents the whole night, and I just let my guard down because I got too tired being on defense.

The next day, during recess, I sat on the swing doing nothing, all bored. Lately, for the whole entire week, propaganda posters had been posted up in the hallways promoting me and promoting Kirsten. People were choosing sides against each other and trying to convince people to come over to theirs. Best friends quickly became enemies. It was all a battle of whether Colin or Kirsten was telling the truth. People were ripping off the posters of their rivals from the walls during class changes. As I walked down the hallway in the mid-afternoon, I was pulled aside and dragged into a corner by somebody's hand.

It was a random girl that I didn't even know or heard of before. Of course, everyone has heard of me after this whole thing and in previous circumstances that date back to who recalls when? Oh well. She was blocking my way out.

"Did you break-up with Kirsten yet?" she asked. "I-uh…" I started but she forced me to lean forward with her hand on my back which I had no idea got there.

She kissed me and I grimaced immediately because I tasted something sugary and sweet with a strong aroma. It was lipstick.

I broke apart from her and fled the scene quickly and swiftly.

I passed by a person who was trying to reach into somebody else's locker and slam it so the owner couldn't get his things. "Give me gum!" he cried. He tried to strike and hit the other guy, but that guy threw up his arms and blocked the blow. "Ow! Ouch!" he started rubbing his arms, and they were all red.

The kid slammed the locker door at the other kid, and he fell. The one who slammed the thing started smacking his victim.

I didn't get to see the aftermath, though.

I passed another similar scenario, but this time it was a feud between a boy and a girl. Somehow, the guy had cracked the girl's mirror, and she was complaining and whining about it at him, saying some nasty things.

At last, I reached English class, and believe it or not, it was Story Day. The teacher read a story about how there was a guy who fell into lava and thought it was the end of his life.

But, when he plunged into the liquid, it was actually water after all!

It was so boring that I fell asleep. I woke with pop music being played out of the radio or something. They don't really do that a lot in school, which was weird, unusual, awkward, not normal, and not typical. I will let you pick the word or phrase.

In Gym, my last period of the day, we played football. I was selected to a team of pretty brawny and fit boys. There were two head coaches and they had to do 'rock-paper-scissors-shoot!' to decide who would go first. The winner picked me right away without hesitation or second-thought. I was selected right off the bat because everybody knows that I am good. They know that I would crush and destroy everyone else, and rule the field. The other team groaned because they knew they were going to lose with me against and facing them. The opposite team started and punted the ball. I caught it before a player on that team received it (interception). I pounded my way through, running around players, and making sure I kept a good distance from each one. It wasn't that easy. I was one of the fastest, and that was good. But I never won the championships in track and field, though, which didn't make sense according to me and in my own opinion and belief.

Players couldn't catch up with me as I zoomed by, making a bunch of twists and turns along the way.

And then, I entered the Touchdown zone.

My team congratulated me and were yelling and screaming very loud. They patted my back and surrounded me. I was used to this. The other team looked and appeared gloomier and glummer than ever. "Colin! You are a legend! You are a beast! You are a savage!" my team chanted proudly and boastfully. I didn't even need to pass once. I was that amazing. I was grinning, seeing people rise in the stands. I heaved my fists in the air as everybody hurried towards me.

Then, I spotted a group of guys arise from below the bleachers. Kirsten was their boss and was giving out directions and instructions. It was pretty ironic that a girl was commanding a group of boys to do stuff. The guys didn't argue. They did as told.

It was dismissal already.

But when I tried to walk off the football field, Kirsten's guys blocked me and my own crew of guys.

"You are not leaving without a fight, Colin."

I shrugged it off. "As you say, bro."

My crew collided with theirs, and there was a lot of tossing around of backpacks and other school supplies being used as weapons. I didn't need to fight because somebody was always defending me all the way back to school as we drove them back to the building.

People were swarming all around me. There was too much action going on. We got close to the pick-up and buses area where there were many engines roaring and vehicles whirling and driving around.

Then, I saw a throng of teachers fighting their way through my army and one got ahold of my arm and clenched it so hard that I sputtered and gasped in pain, grimacing.

They brought me to the front of the school where all the activity was going on, and I was obvious and the center of attention. Then, I saw a familiar face—Kirsten's dad.

He was with what I surmised was his wife because he was standing next to her. They both didn't look relaxed as though I ruined their lives. They gave me stone-hard stares, unblinking, with arms crossed, standing still.

"This was the kid who assaulted your daughter…" the teacher who was clenching my arm announced.

Parents in cars were looking at our way, trying to figure out what in the world was going on there as a source of entertainment.

I could hear my classmates hooting at me.

It seemed like I was on international TV with the whole world watching me. I didn't like it. I didn't feel relaxed or laid-back.

The world was watching my next move.

The teachers made me stand immediately in front of Kirsten's parents. I couldn't bring myself to look at them, while on the grass field. A teacher's hands dug into my shoulders. Nobody said anything for a moment while Kirsten's parents looked-down on me, taking in me. They had all the time in the world. I was impatient to get away from the situation.

"Do not, see me daughter ever again!" Kirsten's dad roared. That was it. That was all they had said.

Kirsten's parents turned around and walked back to the parking lot, towards their car to leave. The teacher let me go.

I headed back towards the building and to the area with all the buses. I boarded my bus: 837. Walking in was a nightmare, with trash strewn everywhere.

I went to the back, the place where I usually sat at to pass time with my fellows. "Yo, what's up, Colin?" my friend Ty, short for Tyler, asked. "Hey!" I replied.

The bus started moving and I heard somebody running toward it as we watched through the window.

Our bus driver Derek didn't notice him and kept driving. We started pointing at the boy trying to catch up. He was sprinting behind the bus now, and I was quite enjoying this. The bus halted at the traffic light and Derek found out and opened the door with the push of a button. The kid, Brady, was breathing so loud that he wouldn't last 5 minutes in a game of hide and seek because of the noise. Again, it was natural after you ran so much, so it couldn't be controlled.

Some boys in the front were trying to shake the bus by wiggling their rear ends. Others were smacking the windows to try to get the attention of those outside and in their cars.

I just sat there like a loner.

"All right, today, I want you all to be respectful of each other, and I can bring you home unlike yesterday. I promise you that because it is my job to do so," Derek told us.

"Got it, Derek!" someone cried.

Then, I saw somebody get up from her seat. It was Kirsten.

A boy next to her, Preston, also got up and they started arguing.

"Why did you say you hated me after everything I have done for you? I even bought you lunch today, all of it! I spent all my money on your crap, and you treated me like this? You said that to me? I am broke now because of you!" he cried and pulled out his phone, showing her the text.

"What do you mean? I didn't send that! I have no idea and no clue who did!" Kirsten fired back angrily. Preston shoved Kirsten away and she went down on the other side of the row of seats.

All day, I was trying to avoid Kirsten or have any eye (physical) contact with her, but seeing what just occurred, I was going to break the reputation. My body just immediately did things I didn't expect it to do at such a calm state.

It was like I released dozens of hormones related to getting mad, and I was certainly boiling and steaming hot right now, probably even on fire when I saw it, inside and out.

"Don't do that!" I got up, ran down the single aisle, and slammed into Preston. Another kid, Cole, started filming us.

Preston scrambled up and I launched myself at his weak body.

I hit him with a great momentum, one great enough to knock somebody out cold. Preston retreated to the back and took out a pencil from his pocket and aimed it at me. "Whatcha going to do, huh? Throw that thing at me?" I challenged him as the words just flew out of my mouth as easily as a waterfall. "Don't make me do this!" he cried.

At last, his patience ran out, and Preston threw it at me but it hit the corner of a seat and bounced out of the open window into North Fields onto somebody's lawn.

"Hey! Who did that?" Derek roared from the front. Apparently, he had been listening. "Stop fighting, you thugs!" "What did he just call us?" Preston cried, but I gave a blow to his head, and now, his face was in a deep color of red, black, purple, and brown combined.

The colors were all mixed together, and now there was a bruise. People all around were chanting, "Fight, Fight, Fight!"

My adrenaline had kicked up so much that now, I was feeling tired and exhausted. Preston was on the floor now, unable to get up and lacking the energy to.

The fight was over, Preston had fainted.

I went over to Kirsten and led out my hand to her to pull herself up. She hesitated, but grabbed my hand and was pulled up.

Kirsten was about to say something when another major episode erupted.

"Attack the school bus driver!" someone yelled, and boys flew from their seats towards Derek.

Derek was driving and he was panicking. He whirled around and drove into somebody's garage. We all fell at the impact.

The owner came out and called for his wife. Derek was badly injured from head to toe with cuts everywhere.

Everybody else was okay, and we escaped through the emergency exits.

One guy left through the hole at the top.

I scooted my way through the floor, lifted and heaved myself up, and squeezed through the window to jump out.

Some kids were too fat, so they were stuck inside. Girls were screaming and freaking themselves out at the calamity.

Once everybody was out, the owners were trying to dislodge Derek from his seat because he got stuck there.

Many took off and ran home, not even bothering to help out. Preston went up to Kirsten and touched her shoulder.

Kirsten flicked her hair and walked away, leaving Preston there depressed. I wanted to pat his back, but couldn't bring myself to do it.

"Oh, you just got rejected!" a kid said to Preston, giggling.

I focused on the scene and saw that the bus had damaged the entire garage plus the two cars inside. One was a pretty luxurious and expensive one. The other resembled a Model T and was rickety and rackety.

I walked home.

My parents asked me how my day went, as usual. I lied about it and said it was "Good!" as usual. I knew I had sent the text to Kirsten about Preston hating her even when he really didn't. They must have known it was me, if possibly not. I just needed to chill. I felt guilty. I needed to take a chill pill.

The next day, things changed. I was told to go to the auditorium by an announcement. I passed by girls who were saying stuff like, "He is so cute, but he is getting braces tomorrow." I knew who they were talking about. It was a guy named Dillan, who all the girls were crazy for.

A random girl came up and started hugging my arm and snuggling with me. I liked her company as I walked down the stairs from the third level to the second one.

I finally entered the auditorium and I saw that there was a small group of people, all of whom were part of my bus.

I suddenly knew what this was all about.

The principal strode onto the stage and said, "We are going to email your parents about this and call them individually if this doesn't end! I do not want to see what happened yesterday ever again!"

Some of us gulped.

"Your bus driver has been seriously injured!" A boy started laughing at these remarks. "You think that is funny?" the principal roared at him, and he stopped.

"Well, it is not funny at all!"

I bet the kid was going to be punished severely, and sure enough, as I left after second period to lunch, I saw the kid with his face all red and crying in a classroom in the corner of the school.

I felt bad for him, so I walked in after checking that nobody was there, even though a security camera must have picked me up, but I knew the teachers were too lazy to keep an eye on anybody. They probably were all sitting in a lounge, sipping hot beverages, and chatting with each other on their break times at the front office. Just maybe.

I knelt behind the teacher's desk and immediately heard footsteps. I winced and found a little hiding spot under the desk where I could fit. An adult entered and the sobbing kid got his act together and gave my secret and hiding place away, both!

"Colin, what are you doing here? What aren't you at lunch?"

I gave the teacher a quick "Sorry" to get out of the situation and sped all the way to the cafeteria. There, I saw my school mates smashing plates and trays of food into the face of the person next to them, also squeezing bags of sauces out everywhere.

A mean kid spat in my face, and I could tell he just finished eating.

Some people were stealing food by putting the item under their tray so the cashier lady couldn't see and charge them.

Everybody just turned into 3 year olds in the cafeteria because they had food all over their clothes, creating stains. The whole place was so unorganized and chaotic. It was messy and very unsanitary.

All the action was in the middle. The boys usually sat in the center tables while the girls were off to the sides to avoid all the dirtiness and uncleanliness created by the boys. There were very few boys who sat with the girls, and I was one of them.

I stepped on a pizza while buying lunch. At least they were not new shoes, because it was really hard to get the cheese off.

Also, I spilled something at my table.

To add onto that, I dropped something too. The lunch monitor made me clean it up and pick it up. He gave me a broom and a sweeper. Some of my friends came over and helped me, but others were booing me.

It was humiliating. Very. I can say that. You wouldn't want to be like me at that moment. Never. You'd change your mind immediately. That I can tell you.

Lunch was over, and a bunch of my girls flanked me all the way up to my next class. "Bye Colin!" they said in their sweet voices, together. My popularity with the girls was growing, which was a good sign.

They all liked me. Or maybe even loved me.

Sometimes, I would even dream about some of them. That was how much I liked them. I would dream about me and them on an island paradise surrounded by miles and miles of water where there was only sunshine, beach, and lush tropical rainforests and jungles. We would dance, paint, create art, make crafts, swim, drink soda, play in the sand, bury ourselves in the sand, and have a good time, mostly. It was supposed to be unceasing, but I would just wake up to find out that it was all fake, and I'd be wishing it were real in my cranky attitude in the morning.

Overall, my view of life was to "Have Fun!" That was all. Only two words. That was my main and only goal, and I tell you, I will achieve it one way or another. Right now, it was not even close to being exciting. I desperately needed a change in my life to break the old traditions and replace them with fresh new ones. My life was depending on it, the change. I would dream about that too.

All in all, I wanted to live the American Dream, to live in a massive house that I liked, own a race car that would get everybody's attention, get famous, become a multi-millionaire, and have a lot of girlfriends, if future holds it. I wanted girls to fall for me right when they see me because I was hot (on fire) and attractive. I was tending to think about the future often and what would become of me. I wanted to become rich and famous. But now, I wasn't getting anywhere to that. So, I was kind of concerned and worried about myself. I was the issue here. Extremely, to be exact. How would I end up? I would ask.

I had to deal with people who would ask stuff like, "Dude, what was that for?" even when I hadn't done anything that would even harm them. Maybe they found it annoying, but I would never know because I was not them.

Then came period change.

I passed by a few girls commenting at each other's appearances. "Do you like my new fabulous look?" one asked courteously and expectantly. "You look so pretty!" her friends said admiringly with a hint of jealousy. "Oh look! It's Colin!" They came over and surrounded me as usual.

I passed by guys who were giving me evil glances even though they were trying to not let me see them. The girls didn't notice, but I was observant.

Ricky, one of the few guys who looked up to me, approached me and suggested, "What about we go to the bowling rink after school today, all right?" This was different, because we usually went with a large group. But it was a perfect excuse to have some fun.

As I said.

Chapter Nine: Bowling!!!

Ricky and I went in the evening. It looked like a nightclub. We were assigned a lane and Ricky scored a strike firsthand. I went and mine's fell into the gutter. "Dude, you suck!!" Ricky slightly shoved me at the side sarcastically. I grinned to respond. He went again, and this time it went straight in an unwavering line and he scored yet another strike.

"I am actually not that bad…" I said and rolled. The ball hit the pins and I was left with a split. I rolled again and the side of the ball scratched the pin, and it twirled. But it just stayed put and didn't collapse. "Ha!" Ricky said. He went at his and forgot to aim. The ball looked dangerously close to the gutter, but it rebounded and curved slowly and gradually the other way while going straight at the same time. He knocked out all the pins.

"What? That is impossible!" "Well, you just saw it, and there you go, I'm a master," he bragged. I made a spare, which I thought was pretty good already. After that, when it was my turn, I ran too far in and slipped on the glossy and waxed lane. Ricky helped me up, and told me to not do that ever again. "I was scared for you!" he admitted.

"I was afraid to death that I would need to call the ambulance and rush you to the hospital, the emergency room. You freaked the freak out of me, bro!" Ricky continued.

I blamed my rental shoes. There were too loose, as compared to tight. Also, my laces kept breaking apart from the knot probably because they were over-worn and old.

We had consumed too much sweets, so we started going wild.

Ricky ran right into the lane towards the pins and slid, kicking them down. There were a lot of people there, so we weren't that obvious. But after a few times, everybody was watching us, and that was what we needed most. We were instantly yelled at by the clerk.

The clerk ran out of patience and the police stomped in, arresting us! They handcuffed our hands behind our backs, and the metal dug into my skin. It would probably leave a deep mark.

We were escorted into the police car with everybody watching us. They locked the door in the back so we couldn't escape.

Ricky tried to bribe them. "Okay, what about this? Here's the real deal, I give you three packs of gum to let us go."

"That's it, nothing else, that simple, all right? Is that a yes?" Ricky asked. "Well, that's a no!" the cop replied.

"That's sad, that's so mean!" Ricky acknowledged. "You bet it is, because you brought it upon yourselves!" the cop said.

"You could have said yes!" Ricky fired back. "Shut your mouth slit..." the cop cried back. "You shouldn't be talking."

They were shaking their heads like they didn't want to be here and would have done anything to be somewhere else. They chatted about us having teenager problems. "Look, we understand completely and clearly about your age. We were once your age, and believe me, I wasn't so pretty..." the cop told us.

We entered the police station and waited in a white blank room for what seemed like hours as they contacted our parents. My parents came over, and from the moment they walked through the door, they refused eye contact with me. "Son, your parents were horrified at the news when I called them, and that's not good. They couldn't believe it. Not a word. Look at what you've done to them! You are such a bad kid to them. I bet they feel very sad they raised you to become like this." the sheriff told me to try to make me feel shameful.

I didn't feel shameful at all! Well, maybe a tad, but I gave the officer a thumbs-up with both hands so he would leave and not oversee what was going to happen now with my parents, and what nasty conversation was going to occur between me and them. I was alone without any help. Ricky was taken to his own parents in a different room.

"You son was taken in for misdemeanor in a bowling rink. The manager of it is expecting you to pay a fine after finding cracks in one of the lanes. Do you hereby accept him back as your biological son under law?" the officer asked. No, I thought, maybe that was the answer. Both yes and no was a bad answer because I was clueless about what to do next.

I was at a crossroad waiting for my parents to open their mouths. The police released me and I walked behind my parents out of a waiting room full of magazines sprawled on tables and elongated couches full of people. I sat in the back and my parents didn't talk to me the whole way the car. They were talking to each other and saying stuff like, "We need to talk some sense into him" and "He is approaching his teenage years, what you think we should do?" Then mom looked at me through the mirror. "Are you kidding me, Colin? This is totally unacceptable."

90

"He has a teenage problem," dad spoke into mom's ear. "He keeps on failing…it is normal," dad added. "Not if you keep making mistakes," mom chided. I was so pissed that I yanked the seatbelt off my body so it wouldn't hold me still, opened the car door while the car was moving, and rolled out. I hit a curb and got up, running. My parent's car stopped a block away and they got out, looking terrified, confused, shocked, and mad at the same time. They went after me as I tried to escape.

I ran for another several blocks before being sprayed on by a neighbor's holes and sprinkler, and tripping on somebody's leg. Apparently, my parents had contacted ahead of time their friends because they knew I was headed towards them. My parents caught up and my dad took my collar and started dragging me back the way we came from. His grip was tight, and it hurt. When we got back, our car was gone! Mom called the same sheriff station and told them everything so they wouldn't get suspicious. Then, a manhunt was officially on for our car-jacker.

We had to call a cab to take us home, and when I got into my room, I just collapsed on my bed and fell asleep.

Chapter Ten: The Changes

The next day was Friday. One more day till the weekends!

A girl was saying something like, "Sheryl, Frankie is getting braces tomorrow!" "I know!" Sheryl nodded.

Frankie was probably the most popular boy who got along with both genders in my grade. Even many kids in seventh and sixth grade knew him too. I was probably ranked #35 most known in the entire school.

At recess, a dog was there running around and licking people's legs. "Why is that there?" somebody cried. "I think it ran away from a farm or something," I told him.

My friend Joey was by my side. He was a good observer, and was studying and watching the dog with sharp eyes.

Mulch was on the ground everywhere.

I organized a game of dodge ball and capture the flag. Many boys went down hard with the balls striking them. Somebody stretched out their hand to tag me before I hopped and stomped over the border line of the territories of the two teams in capture the flag.

In dodge ball, people were randomly throwing the balls.

Everybody was missing but me.

"Aim, guys!" I cried. I thought about merging the two games together, but that would be a pretty bad idea.

The opposite team had a strong shooter and kept taking down and smiting my teammates. They didn't stand a chance. Also, everybody was afraid of getting hit because the force of the balls hurt a lot when you did.

"Don't be afraid of the ball!" I shouted.

Then, recess was over.

Our third period teacher brought us bad news. "You will not have any recess anymore because we believe you all need to grow up." "But we are just having fun!" a kid interrupted. "Yeah," I agreed. "This applies to the whole grade," our teacher said. "We, the grownups, have decided." "No way! You can't do that and take this away. What are we going to do? Watch the seventh and sixth graders play outside?" I cried. "No, recess will be replaced with a time to do homework, why not? We are doing you a favor," my teacher responded coolly. People groaned.

"How can this be? How can that be?" someone stood up and spoke. "Come on, it is not as bad as you think, and please, sit down!" my teacher demanded.

When we left the class, we were all shaking our heads.

Monday arrived, and we were angry at not having recess anymore. So, we organized riot teams.

"It is time to make some trouble," a guy named Lawrence said. "Yeah!" everyone answered.

We hid against the wall of the side of the school, and when the sixth graders went out to recess, we spotted no teachers.

"Now!" somebody ordered.

We ran out to the back and the sixth graders screamed, leaving the playground and basketball court.

But then, we saw movement inside the building towards the back. "Retreat!" I cried. We all scrambled behind bushes.

But I was a bit too slow, being in the front.

It kind of looked like I was the leader.

And I was too late when the first teacher saw me trying to hide.

An announcement came up.

"Colin Shaker, please report to the principal's office immediately, for further notice. No excuses!"

I was taken to the front office and they showed me a footage of the incident. "Was anybody else with you?" the principal asked. I knew that if I gave it away, I would be bullied the next few days. So, I made myself be accountable for the whole thing. "No," I answered, sounding truthful, and they took it. "All right, then. We will be contacting your parents through email or phone for this. We will call home, then. You are suspended until further notice for the rest of the week until you get yourself back into the right mind. Go reflect on your mistakes. This has happened too many times. No more encouraging you to be better. You are ultimately beyond cure," the principal said.

They put me in an empty classroom with nobody but myself for company. "Stay in your seat, we have a surveillance camera watching you," a teacher told me strictly.

I just read posters the whole time, along with studying designs around the room (the very small ones) and daydreaming. The boredom was torturing me all the way to death. This was severe suffering. It was killing me.

The designs were those that weren't so obvious or eye-catching. I thought of the mall and how my fellow classmates (especially the girls) bought clothing that would get people's attentions (those of the boys). The boys always were afraid of how the girls looked at them. They would always buy clothing that had bright colors. They all wanted to look cool and fit in. Nobody wanted to be left out. Not at this age.

Girls were often more carefree, and the boys were more hardcore.

For example, one time, a few guys put whole bags of barbecue sauce mixed with ketchup on a napkin and came over to my table. They seized my lunchbox and wiped it everywhere with the napkin.

I kind of over-reacted.

I chased them down the hallways and around the whole school. The teachers tried to stop me, but I toppled them over. It all ended when we got too tired and forgot about it.

I just gave up because I was facing the kid with the award of "Fastest Guy." He has since been dating the "Fastest Gal" which is definitely no surprise. But the things is, he never gets tired as he runs. He can run for many miles without stopping because it was his innate.

Another time, these boys poured water over the railing onto the landing between the first and second floor. I didn't know that yet. When I went down the stairs, they just stood on the side, which was suspicious. Water was hard to see, and because I was in a hurry to catch up with my friends, I slipped and fell all the way down the second half of the stairs.

The guys were laughing by then and quickly left the scene. Too bad there were no cameras in the stairwells.

My new jacket (a day old) had been soaked in the encounter.

Back to the incident involving barbecue sauce and ketchup. Some of the teachers had to go to the hospital because of brain damage. So, I felt pretty bad.

At lunch, food was being thrown from table to table, and kicked everywhere. This was something done every day.

After school, a group of girls forced me onto their bus as I was hurrying towards mine. Boys were walking out of the way as if wondering why on world they did this to me, and not themselves. I was feeling kind of nervous as I sat in a swarm of them.

The bus stopped and we left straight into a house where there didn't seem to be any adults at that moment. I made a mental note to my parents telling them to not worry but relax because I was coming home soon.

Or maybe I would not be coming home at all, but I wasn't going to say that. Besides, I don't think they got it after all.

Inside, the girls were crazily all over me. They painted both my fingernails and my toenails with all sorts of colors. They never asked my permission but just got to work, setting me on the couch because they knew I would not protest, obviously. It was a great opportunity to *bond* more with them and spend time with them. Especially one of a large group.

Somebody rang the doorbell and a girl went to the front. I could hear, "Can I come in?" from a guy and then, "You're so annoying! Stop! Don't talk to me!" and she slammed the door in the boy's face.

"Who was that?" I asked. "It was Dylan. Sometimes, I really hate him," some girl off to my left said.

"Yeah, he's not even cool *or* cute, I mean, who even likes him?" some girl off to my right agreed.

"He's so lame! All he does is walk around the school carrying his stuff. I see him just sitting in the back corner. He's always alone. He is not popular, unlike Colin here, right Colin?" the girl asks me.

"Yeah," I replied, but it didn't come out too strong. I felt bad for Dylan, but I couldn't let them know that, or else I would be put in the same category.

The next day, I decided to give Dylan some company and sit at the desk next to his. Boys looked behind themselves and shifted gears, surprised. "Is that Colin sitting with Dylan? No way! He would never do that!"

"Well, he just did!" some guy interjected.

Then, Dylan started getting mad and screamed at me. "What did I do wrong?" I cried and quickly left my desk, when at the same time, the teacher walked in.

"Colin! Colin, what was that about? What were you doing? I will send you to the dean and call her!" my teacher yelled. "No! You got it wrong. I can explain!" I shouted back.

My classmates were surely watching the show, leaving no part unwatched and not taking even a single glimpse away.

Their eyes darted back and forth between us whenever one of us started talking. And, the conversation didn't end there, that I can tell you for sure.

They were grinning.

And, I lost the battle, again.

My teacher put somebody in charge of the room as he took me to the library, for some reason. I was put on of the couches.

Four girls walked past the library and saw me through the window.

They waved, and I waved back.

My classroom was probably all ruined by now, since a kid was put in charge, and I knew that kid—he wasn't one of those pretty ones. I never liked him, not a single bit. Then, the vice-principal appeared and arrived.

"We are going to make you write an essay for your punishment about how you think you can make yourself a better person. And you have to get it approved to leave the library, got it?" the vice-principal asked me.

"Yes, I always do…" I answered.

They had also notified my parents and I saw them walk through the library. I quickly ducked and started making my way through the maze of shelves.

"Hey! Where did Colin go?" the librarian called, who was in charge of watching me and making sure I wouldn't try to escape.

I peered around a shelf and saw my vice-principal talking to my parents about stuff like I needed a better behavior because I was so disruptive, and that I needed counseling one on one, and me acting out too much because I was triggered by something.

I was eavesdropping every little word.

My vice-principal also said stuff like if my parents needed help, they could always call school if they wanted. That was it for me. "Hey! He's right there!" the librarian who had been searching for me cried. I darted from my spot and revealed myself.

Grown-ups chased me. Some tripped over the door-stopper and bump. "Get him!" I heard someone cry.

But as I ran around the corner, a group of adults caught me as I whammed right into their enormous bodies.

"What do you think you are doing here?" one asked.

"Stay put!" the librarian cried after them.

I was trying to fight my way through. But they were gripping my wrists, and I couldn't kick because I was held in place firmly and strongly. I was writhing.

"Again, what are you doing here?" another asked me.

"Getting away," I responded truthfully.

My parents and the librarian caught with me now, panting.

"You," the librarian pointed, "will have consequences…"

I had a chance to stare into the ruthless eyes of my parents, and my own were watering. It was to look at them, especially right now and at this instance.

They had saw who I truly was with their very own eyes. There was no more keeping the secret of being that good boy every parent wants. It was over.

This had planned-out my future and mutualistic relationship with my parents. They would see me in a different light now. I would be more disciplined because I was lacking any. No good. Very bad.

Totally bad. Completely bad. Perfectly bad, just how bad luck wanted it to be like. Bad luck had struck up a target and a home run with this one.

"His misdemeanor must not be tolerated. We have had enough, you know? We do not desire nor wish for more!" the librarian announced straight-up to my parents.

"We are sorry for this. We take responsibility and account for our son's actions. But you must know that he is a teenager. He is undergoing a rocky and turbulent time in his life, for whatever reason. We hope he would not bring you pain anymore.

My parents took my arms and dragged me all the way out of the school and into their car. My friends were watching me.

They were smiling at the sight of me and went to others to share the news. It was down-right embarrassing in all matters. You wouldn't want to be me right now, trust me.

I am the only one who knows how it feels, not you, or anybody else.

My parents screamed at me the whole way home and I just looked out of the window and kept my expression blank so that it would be unreadable. They had gotten their car back after the police found and arrested the guy who had stolen our car. I almost hoped he got away with it so my parents wouldn't be able to come in the first place. It was a dirty thought. But that was how I felt, I mean emotions are natural.

It wasn't my fault, not at all! I went to school the next day and a horde of girls pulled-me forcefully to their table at lunch. It was any guy's dream, and I was struck lucky.

"Colin, did you know Hailey here is now dating Gabriel Turner? She used to date Reed Hadsell, but he was dumped because they got into an argument..." a girl named Sophia said. "Yeah, Reed is crying himself out now," Lexi, another girl, added. "He must have lost a piece of his heart," Lin told me. "He might have even lost a piece of his mind also."

Then, a girl named Riley barged in.

"Wait, no way, Gabe and Hailey are actually dating?" Riley asked. "Yeah," Adrianna answered her. "Why not?" Kelsey asked. "They don't go together, that's the point," Adrianna argued back. "They don't match," Ava pointed out.

"All right, I get the point," I said.

I got up and they were like, "Colin, don't leave! Why are you leaving us?" and I was like, "I will be right back."

I decided to give it a try with some boys, and I walked towards them. One kid, named Ryan, greeted me and welcomed me.

"People say you like Julia, do you?" Ryan asked as I squeezed and squished in between the bodies of him and somebody else I knew. I told you, I knew everybody.

"Of course! But, who told you?" I asked. "I can't tell you that, the person who told me this made me promise I wouldn't tell you," Ryan responded.

"Oh come on! I'm your friend. Just tell me! Just tell me if it's a boy or girl..." I begged. "Ok, it is a girl..." Ryan replied. "By the way, people also said you like Morgan too."

"What the heck? How?" I cried. "It's possible," Ryan shrugged like this was normal and totally typical. It wasn't to me.

He was grinning now.

Then, a girl named Mackenzie, or Kenzie, tapped me on the shoulder. She was cool and serious, unlike the others.

"What?" I asked.

"Another girlfriend, have you had enough, Colin?" Ryan rolled his eyes. "I wish I could be like you, you know. I really wish so." "Hey you, shut up!" Kenzie cried at Ryan. Ryan looked away to engage in a different conversation, but I knew he was still listening to me and Mackenzie. For your information, I always tried hard to stay away from really inappropriate people.

"Will says he wants to see you..." Kenzie told me. "Which one?" I asked. "There's only one!" she replied.

I was taken to Will and he whispered into my ear as others tried to eavesdrop. "I know that you are soft on Kenzie."

"What?" I exploded. "That's it?"

Maybe I was a bit too loud.

"What on the world is going on here?" a lunch monitor walked over. "Nothing, we're all good," I answered her.

"Hey! Don't speak to me like that!" the monitor fired back. That got my blood boiling. "So? So what? What is wrong with that, huh?" I asked. "Do you, have you, got a problem with that?"

The monitor shook his head and believe it or not, started sobbing.

I couldn't believe what I just did. I made a teacher cry, which nobody in the history of the school had ever done. It was like I sprayed pepper spray on his face. But this was different, it was natural. It happened like I flicked the "on" on a switch, automatic and immediate. It was triggered. Other teachers came over and took him away, patting his back and comforting him, which I never got by person. Now I was left all alone with a bunch of eighth graders, seventh graders, and sixth graders. People started clapping, applauding, and saying stuff like, "Colin that was sick! That was extremely lit!" I nodded, but I felt like I needed to go to the teacher and say sorry. The lunch monitor was indeed very weak emotionally. I admit, I felt guilty, at least a little.

He had no self-control over it.

I only spoke one phrase, and teachers normally wouldn't care at all about it or take it to heart even a bit.

I bet the teacher was a first-timer in her first year because she was so young, fresh-out of college. I wouldn't be surprised if I was correct. But I couldn't move because I was rooted to spot, immobile. Now the girls would hate me for what I did (at least the gentle ones which I liked).

I messed myself up again. I messed up my reputation again.

Once again (sigh).

"That was pretty fantastic and neat!" a guy came right up next to me. I slapped his face and he fell to the floor, and fainted.

Everybody was either looking at me now or the direction the monitor and the others went. They weren't eating anymore, not one.

"Good job," somebody yelled out.

I got infuriated, and you could see it on my face. "Dude, chill! Calm down! You don't have to get so mad and angry!" this kid told me. I balled up my fists.

"It's all good," I said, and relaxed.

This was the last straw. I'd gotten into trouble enough! That was all I was going to have, final. Mark my words!

"I bet you just broke up with many girls, probably every single one," Ryan came to me. "Leave me alone. Get yourself away. I don't want to see you. I need to think," I said through gritted teeth and honestly.

I needed some breathing room, for real.

So I left the cafeteria and once I left it, it escalated back into the loud and noisy area where they were all talking about me.

I wanted to leave the school, but just wandered the hallways. Ryan caught up with me but I just shooed him away.

"It's okay, man! Don't be so touchy! You're so touchy!" Ryan said. "No! I'm not, now stop!" I yelled back.

I punched the wall even though a surveillance camera was there, watching me. My hand hurt.

"You're a good friend, Ryan!" I said. "What, why? That is unrelated. That is way off topic!" he replied.

I repeated the same thing.

I had to say it even though he might think I was weird. There was always limited things to say, which keeps me silent. I was unlike those who talk way too much.

"Wow, look at who is in front of us!" a female voice said behind me. I turned around and there was Evelyn and her friend Elena.

"Why are you guys just walking around the hallways? It doesn't make sense," Elena asked. "You don't make sense…" Ryan told her back, which was pretty rude.

Now, I was left with no friends, and those who actually were, were yelling at each other. A few teachers strode up to me.

"Come on, man. She just got here a while ago. You can't be like that to her," my Science teacher told me politely.

"Why take advantage of her, out of so many others?" my history teacher asked me. "Why do that? Why do such a thing that cruel?" he added, shaking me up a bit.

I wasn't going to tolerate this pep talk. It didn't look like it was going to end soon. I wasn't going to get out, at least until eternity would be over, which was most likely never, to be honest with you.

Ryan came to me and said something completely random. "You know Kai? He sucks at soccer, I tell you. One time, he hit the pole of the field goal with his own leg as he tried to kick the ball in and lost it. He even shot into the wrong goal once, his own!"

"Ryan! Do you want to get into trouble too? Where did you come from anyway? Don't disturb us or we will phone home for you and tell your parents," my history teacher said. "Ok…" and he walked away, down the hall. It was hard watching him go, my only support and help.

Now I was on my own again.

Against grown-ups.

With no good way out that wouldn't involve hurting the teachers, because I was capable of doing so and not afraid to.

I'd get into some serious trouble. "I know you guys very well because I've met you for so long, you know. I totally understand," my history teacher said. I didn't think that.

I was finally let go and went home that night. I stared at myself in the mirror to see if I was in fact actually that handsome to all the girls. I was trying to figure out which facial features stood out for them.

Or was it my sleek and smooth body? Nobody would ever know the answer to that for sure.

I lay on my bed, wanting to travel around the world and see things, not just to get stuck in this place. I wanted to be a singer, not a mad scientist like my very own parents. At least they didn't get the news concerning my insubordination in school once again.

I wanted to walk out while everybody tried to get even the slightest glimpse of me. I wanted to walk out where everybody would fight for the best position to look at me. I wanted to walk out with hundreds of cameras pointed at me and clicking. I wanted to walk out with people cheering me on. I wanted to walk out with girls being stunned at my appearance.

But sadly, all these were just wishes and good dreams yet to come true. I couldn't accept a "never" for these, though, as hard as it was. A never just wouldn't fit, ever.

"Colin?" my mom came in, closing the door behind her. "I just applied you for a science school for next year…" "Wait, you mean I am leaving Tony Craig Middle School forever?" I asked, suddenly aware of the matter.

"No, not yet. They are asking for you to take this test and submit three teacher recommendations. I am doing this so you could become a good scientist one day, you know. It is for the best of you. I want to train you like this. So I did it," mom explained.

"What? You can't do that! I don't want to! I am not ready!" I totally freaked out. "Oh come on, just give it a try, would you? Make me proud for once! You don't have to get in, even though I really want you to," mom responded. "Just challenge yourself for once. It is good for you. Your mom wants the best for you," she added. "But I don't want to even be a scientist in the future! I will never ever…" I cried. "You got it all wrong, Colin. This is a good opportunity. You just don't get it, don't you? Trust your mom, she has been through this before. Even dad agrees," mom answered.

"Well, I don't care about whatever you think," I cried back. "If I don't want to, then I don't need to or have to!" I added. "No, Colin. Your dad and I have already made our decision and submitted your admission. We can't cancel it, too bad," mom said. "So you are going to pull me out of school and then I would need to start all over and make new friends?" I asked. "Yes," mom replied clearly.

"After this school year ends, if you make it, you will move over and relocate to that science school. You will then attend it too. Also, you have to say why you want to go to that school and explain. I have high expectations and expect it to be good before it is submitted," mom told me. "I have had enough! I don't even want to go to that school, how am I going to write about that even when I don't feel like it? Even when it doesn't come from my heart and inside me? Do I really have to make it all up?" I fired back at mom questionably.

"I am sure you won't need to. I know you can do it, Colin. I believe in you and have faith for you as your mom. I am sure dad thinks the same exact thing…" mom spoke to me strongly and confidently. "How do you know?" I questioned. I, on the other hand, wasn't so courageous nor prepared for what was about to come or would come. I didn't care about it still and anyway. Besides, it wasn't one of my very own priorities. And never would it be. I know it does and might sound kind of harsh, but that was how I felt about and towards it now. I would have felt anxious and nervous or maybe even pressured and stressed. Mom always wanted to me to be the best at everything and above all. Mom keeps thinking I never make her proud.

That is probably what troubles her. She says I don't challenge myself enough and am always staying in my comfort zone and not expanding my boundaries and limits at least a little.

Mom didn't care about my relationships with all the girls at my school and how much I treasured and cherished them. I didn't want to lose contact with them. I held them close to heart. That would be very sad for me, I admit. Mom and I quarreled all night, and we both were determined to not sleep until one of us won the heated and intense debate. The conversation and exchanges took forever. We tried to convince and persuade each other with both our opinions.

By the time it was over, the sun had risen again. Dad had just woken up from his deep and undisturbed sleep.

Me and mom had dark spots under our eyes from the lack of sleep, and we barely could move or talk because of the drowsiness.

"Can I not go to school today and sleep?" I asked. "Colin, you know the answer to that! Of course you cannot. It was your fault you didn't sleep," mom said as she went to sleep on my bed. "Go to school, boy. Go to school, kid," she ordered me strictly.

"But I am extremely fatigued!" I cried. "Hurry, you are going to miss the buss," mom murmured with her eyes closed. She started sleep talking. I hurried out, not even caring to wash my face or eat breakfast. Dad bear-hugged me on the way out so much I thought I would lose all the air and oxygen from my lungs leaving my body through my throat. My mouth was wide open too. It was unexpected and caught me by surprise. He kissed the top of my head and let me go and leave through the side door. Usually I left through the back door and garage, but this time, I felt different. The doors were closing as I sprinted towards the bus and made it in just in time.

And I had a bad night, staying up the whole and entire time.

A girl tried to corner me and force me to kiss her on the lips, somehow. Normally, I would have let her, or maybe I did. I don't know. I was too slow processing, so I wasn't really sure what was going on. Everything was a blur today. I couldn't figure out what exactly was going on most of the time today. I wasn't productive and made many mistakes. I couldn't focus nor concentrate on just about anything there was, which was a lot. That night, dad and I made a secret meet from mom.

Dad got out of his master bedroom and walked downstairs at midnight, so did I. He'd bought a lot of junk food and stowed it away so mom wouldn't find them. We had a midnight snack, in other words, a silent party full of food. It was fun.

The next day, I let another girl kiss me when nobody was looking. The same girl yesterday who had tried to kiss me came up to me and saw what I did with the other girl. She broke up and started crying, walking away. The girl I kissed reluctantly left me there.

I kissed another girl while we sat on a bench the same day and she asked if I would go out with her. My face flushed and turned red. I was at a loss of words while she waited for my response nervously. Usually, it should be the boy who asks the girl, so this was outright different.

I have an interest in what other people are doing so I went to check them out. It wasn't anything exciting or interesting, which is always how it is.

That night, dad and I had the same silent party thingy. Mom caught us this time. I was put to sleep shortly afterward as she yelled at my dad and gave him a piece of her mind.

I bet he wasn't going to do it again to risk the same experience and talk from mom. I fell asleep and then I woke, seeing a shadow on my curtain. I froze, fearing I would trigger it if I moved even a muscle. My heart was pounding. I was scared to death. I wanted to get out of there. Then the door of my room opened slowly and I screamed, but there was no sound.

This was a nightmare. I saw a humanoid shape and figure standing there, coming towards me. And then, the lights flicked on, and of course, it was mom sleepwalking. That was her gift, she was good at doing that. I always hated it. You never know which night she was going to creep into your room and when.

This was scary enough. Another night, I felt somebody or maybe even something touch and grab my foot. One second it was there, and the other, it was gone without a trace, mark, or sign it had ever been there. But I was sure about it. Then, morning arrived! Mom never knew when she was actually sleepwalking, which totally sucks.

I sat with my friends Ashwin and Cameron at lunch. A guy named Carl came over and said, "Yo, man. Dude, let's get this straight. You…like Mallory, don't you?"

"You're messed up!" I cried at him.

He turned his back to me and started walking away back to his table, looking around a couple times to see my reactions.

"He does have a point there, I mean, we see you walking around with her everywhere during period change," Ashwin pointed out. "When did I do that, like ever?" I asked agitatedly. "You know what? I side with Ashwin on this too," Cameron informed me.

My friends had let me down. They weren't loyal enough.

As I walked through the halls, Ashwin appeared next to me. "Did you know Frankie asked the dean if she would go with him to prom and homecoming?"

I stopped in my tracks, jaw-dropping.

"You're lying, I know you are…" "No! I'm not! I'm telling the truth!" Ashwin responded. "Plus, she said to Frankie that he shouldn't say that, but she didn't say no to his request!" "Oh wow…" I answered. I went to class and a few girls were chattering over one of their boyfriends. A girl from the group got a whiteboard and started scribbling onto it. Then, she showed it to all the other girls. It read: Aiden + Allison = Puke. "Oh, stop it!" one of them replied.

She snatched the whiteboard eraser from the girl who had written it and wiped the words off clean.

"Don't do that!" a girl named Celine cried. "You are so retarded!" Ashley told Celine, which made her mad.

"I am not!" Celine cried back.

"No, you are...face it. That's the dark truth," Ashley retorted. "No, it's not! You're wrong!" Celine shook her head. "Sometimes, you are just so aggressive," I told this to Celine with a smile, because I kind of had a crush on her, not saying that I was soft on her, but maybe. Then, my long-time friend Tracy appeared, along with another familiar face, Sharon.

I looked to my side, and there was Addy just casually sitting on her desk like the teacher had not told her to not to do that a moment before. Besides, she barely cared about anything at all. "Are you in this?" Addy asked me. "Cause you're being over-powered by two gang of girls that have stirred up a fight," she added before I could respond. "I glimpsed around and realized I was in between the two groups of girls who were looking for a verbal fight. Normally, they would have went off with it, but with me, they couldn't.

I was in their business, in the way, and in the middle of it all. "So Colin, which side you going to choose?" Addy asked. She figured I was just caught in the situation and am on a neutral team. I gave the dumbest reply in all of history when men answered to women.

It was: "I don't know." I felt like the reply wasn't cool enough, and I wasn't so bright the remainder and rest of the day. I felt like a complete dork. An absolute jerk.

It sure didn't impress any girls, and that was worse than picking a side to be on, because whatever side I were to pick, it would be more supreme than the other with me.

When I saw Kirsten during the day from afar, I knew she was the one, even though she had fooled me.

But hey, nobody was perfect.

Chapter Eleven: The Abduction

The electronic dismissal bell finally rung for the entire school to hear.

I went to my locker, packed up binders into my backpack, and headed outdoors to catch the school bus.

I decided to stalk Kirsten all the way back to her house, which was creepy, but I had a desire to take a risk.

I kept a good distance behind her so she wouldn't feel like she was being followed or trailed by somebody behind.

At the gate, I waited for her to get inside her house first before I revealed myself. Then, I strode up the stairs to the front door, and after taking a deep breath, rang the bell.

Her buff dad appeared, opening the door, wearing a military shirt. I got to my message: "I am really sorry about what I did to Kirsten, but please forgive me, because I really like her…"

"Your name's Colin, right? Get the hell out of here…" he told me. The moment I heard that, I slumped, and turned around to leave.

Defeated, and rejected.

That was my last chance. I had wasted it, or it just didn't work.

When I got back home, mom asked, "What took you so long?" I retreated to my bedroom as usual. "Nothing, it was just some traffic on the road…"

I wanted to cry, wanted to feel helpless.

Another day of school went by, as usual. It wasn't interesting or exciting anymore. It was the same-o.

But after we were dismissed again, I saw Kirsten walk home the opposite way she usually did, which I caught suspicious. Nobody else was paying attention to her, only me. Well, maybe some other guys also. I had to do something, I shouldn't walk away. So I decided to follow her into the unknown.

A truck ran by and stopped in front of her a couple blocks away from school. Now I couldn't see the school at all.

When Kirsten looked as if she was going to look behind her, I scrambled and hid behind a bush even thought I was in plain sight on somebody's lawn. Kirsten never did look behind herself at what was behind her anyway.

Kirsten stopped and seemed to be waiting for something.

The door of the shotgun seat flew open and a guy in a head mask grabbed Kirsten and pulled her into the van. Kirsten lurched and screamed at this as he did so.

I flew into a full-on sprint and made myself go into the trunk of the truck, which was this box double the size of the front.

I quickly hid behind a crate as I heard feet stomp toward the opening in the back. "All clear," a rough man's voice said, and the sliding door slid from the top and locked at the bottom, concealing me in the rectangular box.

I stayed in the box for what seemed like a whole day. I had no idea where I was going, but I knew Kirsten was here too. I was determined to find what those mysterious men were up to and get Kirsten back, somehow.

The truck stopped.

I pushed myself into an empty mini box the size of a bathtub and pulled the rubber lid over my body. I heard the sliding door open. "Take out the things," a guy said.

The men quickly lifted things out of the trunk. A person picked the box I was in up and exclaimed, "Anderson, why is this so heavy?" Shortly after, the boss replied, "Don't be an idiot, they are all heavy…"

"This one seems pretty weird…" the guy said back. "You seem pretty weird for saying that. All that is important now is the girl. I can't wait to sell her to Mexico. We are spending the night at this motel and leaving at 5 am tomorrow morning, now let's go," the boss told him.

I gasped at this. They were going to sell Kirsten as a victim of human trafficking to maybe some drug dealer in Mexico for like thousands of American dollars.

I was taken into a motel room, and then into a walk-in closet.

The door shut, and I could hear the three guys saying, "Let's go get some dinner out there," and went out the door.

The coast was clear. I got out of my box and out the closet. I could hear Kirsten squirming, screaming, and kicking the walls of a bathroom, trying to escape and at least signal to others that she was trapped.

I hurried towards her voice.

I unlocked the bathroom door and scrambled inside, but was met with a fury of whacks. "Colin? Is that you? Why are you here? How…?" Kirsten suddenly looked surprised.

"Thanks for slapping me and thinking I was one of the guys, you are one tough girl," which owned me another slap from her.

Then I looked up and saw that she was bounded in chains and duct tape was wrapped around her wrists and ankles. She was sitting on the floor next to the sink.

"What happened?" I asked.

"Well, I found this guy online and we started texting. He told me to meet him at that place where I was taken and now this. Can you please tell me how you got here?" Kirsten looked at me with surprise.

"Okay, this is kind of embarrassing. I stalked you and went into the back trunk of the truck before it left, now this," I said, and she just nodded as though it was coincidence.

"They are going to sell me to a Mexican man!" Kirsten cried angrily. "I mean, who does that?" she shouted.

"Quiet, they might hear you."

I cupped my hand to her mouth so she wouldn't talk as I took out my phone with the other. I never liked using my data plan when there was no Wi-Fi since it was limited, but now was an emergency.

I dialed 911 and the operator picked up. "Hello?" I said, "Okay, I am in this motel off some interstate highway system. My friend has just been kidnapped and I have found her. Can you track my phone for the cops to come? There are a few guys who seem like they could fight."

I ripped out the duct tape to set Kirsten free and she yelped because I did it too fast. "That hurts! Stop! Don't do that! Careful!" Her eyes shone with fear of pain.

"It's okay, trust me," I assured her.

Then, through the closed bathroom door, I heard the guys come back apparently only 10 minutes later. Had they gotten any food? I didn't know about that.

I heard sirens in the distance and knew it was our time to act.

"Let's go, take the run for it," I ordered. Together, we got out of the bathroom and ran for our dear lives.

The guys jumped at the sight of me from their white-sheet beds and ran after us as we flew out of the motel room and into the open parking lot toward the group of police cars advancing on us. We got to the grass and I pushed Kirsten into one of the police cars while I headed for the next one. Expect that I forgot about a rock the size of my foot ahead of me.

My foot collided with the rock and I went heads-over-heels and crashed my head on the concrete curb. It felt like a gazillion concussions just broke out. I didn't remember what occurred next, not a bit.

Chapter Twelve: The Reunion

I woke up on a hospital bed, not sure what exactly just happened. Kirsten and her parents were there at my side. My parents were there in front of me. They all whooped in joy as they saw me open my eyes.

"He is only suffering from minor injuries, but they would heal in about a week," the doctor said to my parents.

Kirsten's dad patted my shoulder and said, "Thank you so much for saving my daughter, Colin Shaker." To me, those were the best-said words I had ever heard in my life. They meant so much to me.

"No problem, it was an honor," I replied.

"Now let me rest, I need to get well soon," I told everyone, and drifted into a deep sleep, far away from the world.

Epilogue:

I had dates with Kirsten every day after school now, and I was considered her boyfriend after the news broke out in school, even though some guys were still a little bit upset I had stolen her for myself. I had promised them to get them each a girlfriend, but sometimes, you just have to break promises, which makes you highly untrustworthy and unreliable. But who cared now? Now I could go back to normal and chase the American Dream. I have already checked a box on the list, which was getting a girlfriend. I didn't know how long the relationship would last, hopefully for a little while. Next was getting a race car, buying a unique house, getting famous, going on camera, and much more. The new girl, Florence, seemed to be pretty good at fitting in now.

I was proud of her for that.

Kirsten and I went out to a little ice cream parlor one day. We held hands and shared both of out sundaes. By the way, it was a Sunday to begin with. "Colin, you are a remarkable boy," Kirsten said, and we kissed, forgetting about the old times when we hated each other, forgetting about our surroundings, and always looking forward to the riches of the future, the experiences, and what they might bring eventually.

Acknowledgements

I wrote this book from my own experiences in middle school and observations of my schoolmates, their behaviors, and what topics are most popular in the teenage years. This book really informs the reader of the thoughts of a teenager and their desires in an anecdotal way during this period of life. You can see how the struggles of Colin Shaker reflect on being a teenager.

I would like to thank all my peers who encouraged me to write novels in the first place, and who inspired me to do this. I believe God gave me this gift of writing stories for others to enjoy, and also for my own enjoyment. Thanks to all, and see you again next time!

www.ingramcontent.com/pod-product-compliance
Lightning Source LLC
Chambersburg PA
CBHW051847170626
46807CB00003B/1391